Praise for MONSTERS
by Emerald Fennell

'Emerald Fennell's novel *Monsters* is a tremendous, destabilising work of fiction, infusing the mundane with eerie and unsettling darkness. It is written, moreover, in a remarkable tone of voice: Roald Dahl meets Muriel Spark. Astonishing' William Boyd, *New Statesman*

'. . . a mash-up of *Carrie* and *Bluebeard* with a touch of *The Girl With the Dragon Tattoo*, *Monsters* is smart, modern and fresh. This savagely and ultimately bleak tale is not for the faint of heart' *Financial Times*

'Emerald Fennell combines sharp psychological insight with mordant humour to fashion a dark, contemporary fairy tale' *Mail on Sunday*

'*Monsters* by Emerald Fennell is absolutely great. It's about two appalling children, a sinister seaside holiday and a spate of murders.

It's gripping and astonishingly, gleefully dark'
Molly Guinness, *Spectator*

'Emerald Fennell's *Monsters* will delight 12-plus
fans of Edward Gorey, Lemony Snicket and Bret
Easton Ellis; it is a hideously funny account
by a cynical thirteen-year-old girl of a series
of murders in the Cornish town of Fowey.
Sophisticated and suspenseful, it has a view
of parents that adults would be wise to avoid
reading' Amanda Craig, *New Statesman*

'The two kids embark on a blissful summer of
voyeurism, spying and youthful sleuthing of the
most appalling kind. They may not be the Secret
Seven, but they are disturbingly compelling'
Imogen Russell Williams, *Guardian*

'It's very difficult not to overuse the word
"disturbing" to describe this book . . . *Monsters*
is a challenging novel for teens that is a
well-balanced combination of shocking,
thought-provoking and gruesomely entertaining
writing' We Love This Book

MONSTERS

MONSTERS

EMERALD
FENNELL

HOT
KEY
BOOKS

First published in Great Britain in 2015 by
HOT KEY BOOKS
4th Floor, Victoria House, Bloomsbury Square
London WC1B 4DA
Owned by Bonnier Books, Sveavägen 56, Stockholm, Sweden
www.hotkeybooks.com

This is a work of fiction. Names, places, events and incidents are either
the products of the author's imagination or used fictitiously. Any
resemblance to actual persons, living or dead, is purely coincidental.

A CIP catalogue record for this book is available from the British Library.

ISBN: 978-1-4714-0462-7
Also available as an ebook

5

This book is typeset using Atomik ePublisher
Printed and bound in Great Britain by Clays Ltd, Elcograf S.p.A.

Hot Key Books is an imprint of Bonnier Books UK
www.bonnierbooks.co.uk

For my family –
Mum, Dad, Coco and Chris

What do two monsters do when they
pass each other in the forest?
 Smile.

(German proverb)

1

Mummy and Daddy

My parents got smushed to death in a boating accident when I was nine. Don't worry – I'm not that sad about it.

Daddy worked in a huge bank in London, with a pretty receptionist and a shiny, shiny marble floor with lots of droopy ferns. Mummy was an artist, but mostly this meant that she hand-made cards for her friends and cried a lot. Daddy said that was what made her an 'artist': all the crying.

They didn't like me very much, or if they did they didn't particularly show it. I don't think they ever really got to grips with the idea of children in general, and me in particular; they yelled at me for doing practically anything. We lived in a swanky flat in Knightsbridge, where everything was cream-coloured and all the glass tables were covered in 'decorative stones' that had all been hand-selected by a man in Somerset. Why on earth they were any better than just normal stones I have no idea, but Mummy always got really cross when I played with them, so I chucked one through a glass window and pretended it was an accident. Mummy was always very worried about the flat – about the window latches not going with the doorknobs, and about the vases from Paris clashing with the curtain sashes from Venice. She spent all day wandering around the rooms, checking for smudges on the walls and fingerprints on the light switches.

Mummy and Daddy seemed angry a lot of the time, but they got especially annoyed when they couldn't get a new nanny for me because all of mine kept leaving and 'word had got around' about me. Honestly! It's not my fault that nannies don't like practical jokes and burst into tears all the time. I don't know why Mummy even needed one in the first place – it's not like she had anything better to do than look after me.

I hardly even saw Mummy and Daddy; they avoided me in our huge flat and they never let me eat with them, even though I was an only child! I had to eat by myself every night at the big shark-skin table in the dining room, while they shouted at each other in the next room about Mummy and her paintings (most of them portrayed Daddy as an evil centaur). Then they would send me to my room, which Mummy had painted grey because the interior decorator told her it would be more sophisticated and I could 'grow into it'. This was obviously pretty pointless given that it turned out Mummy and Daddy would be dead soon and there'd be no time for me to grow into the room anyway.

I'd sit in my grey room, listening to them throwing decorative ashtrays from China at each other's heads, and talk to my imaginary friend Malcolm, who sometimes told me to peel the paint off the walls, and once made me hide some of Daddy's important paperwork from him. Malcolm was great. He had a face on the back of his head. The nannies hated Malcolm. Mummy didn't really like Malcolm either, and wouldn't let me talk to him in front of her, so he used to spit in her drink when she wasn't looking and sometimes wrote horrid words on her paintings. Malcolm always knew how to cheer me up. Then Malcolm went to live with the family next door. I don't think their little girl liked him – she always burst into tears when I pointed out that Malcolm was walking behind her in the hallway.

The Summer of the Smushing, Daddy took Mummy on a posh cruise because they had been fighting even more than usual, this time because of the pretty receptionist at the bank, whose name was Trish but who Mummy called 'that anorexic slut-child' because she was younger and thinner than Mummy. Mummy was obsessed with being thin – it was the thing she was most proud of.

At meal times she only ate peas, one at a time, with her fingers.

Daddy thought that what they needed in order to 'patch things up' after all the Trish business was a lovely, relaxing holiday. It can't have gone very well because halfway to Egypt Mummy jumped off the boat. Daddy dived in to rescue her, but he made a bit of a hash of it because they both got sucked underneath and caught up in the propellers.

A policeman came to my school and told me in the Headmistress's office, with his hat on his lap. I didn't believe him and thought it was a joke for ages. I laughed and laughed until they sent me to the school nurse for some calming-down medicine. Everyone at school was really nice to me for a week, even my enemies, and I got to go to the funeral wearing one of Mummy's old hats, with lots of feathers on it and a veil.

The upside of having your parents chopped to smithereens by a boat propeller and (possibly) eaten by sharks (the police couldn't be sure) is that there is no one left to tell you off and make you go to bed early, and you can eat nothing but pudding for months because no one dares to stop you.

Our big flat got sold and I was sent to live in the country with Granny. Granny is Mummy's mummy, but you wouldn't know it because there are no pictures of Mummy anywhere.

Granny lives in a bungalow in the middle of nowhere because she is allergic to car fumes. I'm not even allowed to talk about cars because it makes Granny feel faint. Sometimes I turn on the telly when I know the car racing is happening, just to see Granny start clawing at her throat and wheezing. As though the fumes could get through the telly! Granny is almost sillier than Mummy was about her phobias, and that really is saying something.

Granny wears only pink and spends hours putting on make-up and doing her hair. I don't know why, because she doesn't ever see anyone but me. Even the postman can't come up to the door because his van makes Granny ill, so I have to walk to the Post Office once a week to collect

Granny's letters, while Granny sits by the window, painted up like a china doll, watching the drive in case a car dares to come down it.

The good thing about living with Granny is that she has no idea about twelve-year-old girls and what they should be reading or watching on the television, so she lets me sit up with her and watch gory films while she picks the polish off her nails and feeds it to her dog, John. John is permanently at death's door but never actually hobbles through it. I'd put him out of his misery but Granny carries him around everywhere with her on account of his only having three legs.

Granny and I both love gory films, and true crime. She has millions of books on the subject, and sometimes asks me to read the really violent bits out loud to her over and over again. She especially likes it if someone has dissolved his wife and poured her down the sink, or cut up a body into bits and hidden it in bin bags. She likes the bit after the murdering more than the murdering itself, and says 'Clever devil' a lot under her breath when someone has thought up a particularly cunning method. I don't know what Grandpa thought about it all – he must have been terrified that Granny was going to put an axe through his head at any minute, with her banging on about body farms and rigor mortis all day long. Grandpa is in a home now, and Granny doesn't visit him any more because he doesn't remember who she is, so she doesn't see the point.

I go to school in the village near Granny's house. There are only seven other people in my class, and my teacher, Mr West, doesn't believe in traditional learning, so mostly we go into the woods and collect specimens or do battle re-enactments in the playground for history. I like Mr West a lot, we all do; he never gets cross no matter how many times you try to stick your hands in the hydrochloric acid in science. Mr West and I are great friends. He always reads my stories and says that I should be a writer one day because of my vivid imagination. I used to go round to his house and knock on the door anytime I liked to show him one of my new stories, or to ask him about something I'd heard in the news, but he asked me to stop doing that. He didn't say so, but I guessed it was because of his wife, who wears enormous jumpers and pink glasses and doesn't like me or my stories. Poor Mr West. I honestly don't know why people ever get married.

It is going to be my thirteenth birthday this summer during the holidays, so everyone at school brought in something they'd made for me in the summer term. This is what we do for birthdays in our school. We aren't allowed to buy anything. Last year Mr West made me a T-shirt with a picture of Vlad the Impaler on it, because I really liked Vlad when we were studying him in history. Mr West drew the picture himself with a special T-shirt pen: Vlad is holding a head on a spike and underneath him it says, 'Vlad to the Bone!' I wear the T-shirt every day. People tease me about it at school now, but I know they're only jealous because my Mr West T-shirt is the best one he's done so far. This year he gave me one with Marie Antoinette on it, with her head through the guillotine. When I grow up I'd like to marry Mr West, and I'll wear the T-shirt and we'll laugh about his old wife and how pointy her face is and how much better I am than her. Someone at school said Mrs West was going to have a baby, and that's why she wears all the big jumpers. That made me really upset and ruined the last few weeks of term. It meant that I was quite rude to Mr West and said something about his wife that I shouldn't have. I think he secretly agreed with me about his wife, but he had to give me a detention for show so that the others didn't start talking about Mrs W's bottom too.

It was a real shame that the end of term was ruined for me. I really like my school but, honestly, sometimes I think it would be better if someone just burned the place to the ground.

2

Summer Holidays

During the summer holidays, Granny always decides she has had enough of me and goes to an island somewhere to drink holy water and watch people get cured, so I have to go and stay with Mummy's sister and her husband in Cornwall.

Aunt Maria and Uncle Frederick own a hotel in Fowey. They inherited it from Uncle Frederick's parents, and it feels as though nothing has been changed since Uncle Frederick's old mum died twenty years ago. It's on the edge of a cliff (slightly over the edge, really, which is probably why it's always so empty), overlooking the town and the estuary. You can see it for miles around, with its peeling windows and rusting iron letters on the front that say THE CLIFF HOTEL. The place is huge, like a mouldy old wedding cake, with fifty bedrooms, all of them with the same matching red curtains and bedspreads, and orange en-suite bathrooms. The whole place smells of dried flowers and burnt egg, and there isn't a nail or picture hook in the entire hotel that doesn't have a few dusty sprigs of old Christmas tinsel caught on it all year round.

Aunt Maria sits in the sickly, lacquered pink lobby, jumping with fright anytime the door opens, while Uncle Frederick handles 'the business side' in his office, which Aunt Maria and I are forbidden to go into in case we mess things up. I've spied on the office quite a few times through the window and I don't know why Uncle Frederick is so precious about it, because he's only reading old classic-car magazines and drinking coffee in there.

Even though I visit them every summer, Aunt Maria and Uncle Frederick are never really happy to see me. Granny says it's because Aunt Maria had a baby the same age as me that only lived for a few months, and so having me skipping about the place makes her sad. I can't imagine Aunt Maria having a baby at all. She's so frail and dry, and jittery, like a moth trapped in a lamp. The idea that she ever had enough blood to grow a baby seems impossible. Uncle Frederick, though, has enough blood for them both – he's throbbing with it and looks as though he might explode at any moment. Sometimes he does. Aunt Maria speaks very softly, in her whispery, moth-like way, and twitches if you say something when she wasn't expecting it. She whispers because she is frightened of Uncle Frederick and doesn't want to attract his attention, even when he's talking to her.

They aren't interested in what I do as long as I keep out of their way, so they give me a door card – which makes a lovely, satisfying bleep when you slot it into the doors – and leave me to come and go from the hotel as I please.

Fowey is a tiny multicoloured town on the estuary, built up the side of a green, green hill and looking out to the sea. It's threaded with fairy lights and pastel bunting and looks exactly like all the tiny watercolours they sell in the Parker and Hulme gift shop. It has an aquarium with a tank full of writhing conger eels, and a mouldy public toilet, which got shut down because of something that happened in there a few years ago.

In the centre of the town, surrounded by a stone wall crawling with yellow roses, is Podmore Hall, the house of the Podmore family, who have owned the town for centuries. For the last forty years the latest Podmore, William, has lived in it. Everyone is terrified of William Podmore. He hardly ever leaves the Hall and no one has seen him for years. He just sends letters in purple ink threatening his tenants over the smallest things, like using the wrong font on a menu or selling a postcard that 'does not befit the nature of the town'. Everyone wonders how he finds all this out, since he never comes into the town. Some people think he has spies, watching and listening and making notes, and then there are the rumours that he has secret tunnels under his house leading into the town centre and that he roams the place at night, inspecting all of the buildings. I always overhear people muttering about him, worrying that they might get on the wrong side of him and get booted out of their homes. It is very important to William Podmore that the town is perfect and that it does not let the 'new world' in, and so Fowey looks exactly as it did a hundred years ago, give or take a few fairy lights.

My favourite shop in the town is the sweetshop, Queen's Confectionery, which is owned by Peter Queen. I like Mr Queen because he lets me stay in his shop for ages just having a look and chatting to him, even if I only ever buy a few pink shrimps. Mr Queen has red, tightly curled hair like a clown and is bent over from years of weighing sweets on his brass scales. He wears embroidered waistcoats and has wet eyes. I think he is quite lonely – his wife died ages ago and he has a yellowing photograph of their wedding day sellotaped to the till, which he spends a lot of time staring at.

I don't think he even likes sweets very much – or, at least, I've never seen him eat any.

I am obsessed with sweets. Granny doesn't let me have sugar, so when I come to Fowey for the summer I usually go a bit cuckoo-crazy for the first few days while I let all the sugar zap around my body. Mr Queen sells every type of sweet you could possibly imagine – the shop is crammed with dusty bottles and jars full of everything you'd ever want: gobstoppers and strawberry laces and cinder toffee and chocolate cigarettes and fairy dust. The window is stacked with bricks of fudge, which Mr Queen makes upstairs in his kitchen. Some of them have been sitting in the window so long they're turning white and have fruit flies stuck to them. I wonder whether if I had some of the window fudge it would make me sick, but Mr Queen is always paying attention, so I can't break off a piece to see. I make do with the Fowey pebbles, which look like the rocks you find on the beach. I keep a bag in my satchel at all times, and click them around in my mouth as I walk around the town.

Sometimes I'll go down and crab by the quay. You only need a bit of bacon and a weighted line and crab net and the crabs just walk right into it and get tangled up. There are so many people crabbing on the quay wall that the crabs must spend their lives being hauled out of the water and poked at and then tossed back in again. You'd think they'd have learned their lesson by now and would just give the bacon a wide berth, especially since some of the smaller children twist off a leg or two before their parents can stop it, but I'm afraid crabs are just idiots – there's no way of sugar-coating it.

When I first started spending the summer in Fowey three years ago, people used to stop me in the street when I was by myself to ask if I was all right and if I had lost my mum, which I had, but not in the way they meant. This year no one has stopped me at all, probably because I am a bit taller and have a short, sophisticated haircut that I did myself in the sink with Granny's nail scissors. Most of the shopkeepers know me now too; I like to go into the shops every day to have a chat with them, just to keep an eye on things. Some of them are friendly, like Margaret and Phillipa Flower, the old, identical twins who own Flowers' Bookshop, and some of them aren't, like Mr Field from Field and Gray's tool shop, who tells me to bugger off.

Most days nothing will happen at all, but sometimes, if I'm lucky, George Brain will drag out his old wooden box, stand on it and start shouting down by the quay. My uncle calls George Brain 'the eyesore', and he certainly is pretty strange to look at, with tufty black hair and a bubbly red nose and drooping green cardigan. George Brain went mad after the clay mine closed and he lost his job, and he starts drinking from the moment the Ship Inn opens until he is too drunk to stand up. If he's not fast asleep by teatime, he'll get up on his box and do one of his speeches about corruption and the closure of the mines and the Podmore family being evil and the smugglers' caves being full of blind mermaids and devil worship and the estuary being home to a huge kraken that feeds on the innocent souls of children while they swim.

I love George Brain. He always has an exciting twist on life in the town. Sometimes it'll be fairies up by St Catherine's Point, other times it'll be poison in the water by Readymoney Cove. The Mayor, Robert Hoolhouse, who wears a blond wig and pastel trousers from the golf shop, keeps trying to stop George Brain from doing his speeches, especially during Regatta Week when all the tourists are in town, but because of free speech, and because George Brain lives in the hills and not in one of the Podmore-owned houses in the town, there isn't much Hoolhouse can do but lump it. I don't know why the tourists would mind it anyway. George Brain's speeches give the town a bit of character, especially when he has drunk too much and has to be sick off the side of the quay halfway through. Now that's entertainment!

Most days, though, George Brain will just pass out round the back of the pub, so there isn't much to do but wander around the town. I'll do my usual round of the shops and maybe pop something into my satchel when a shopkeeper isn't looking, or I might go and talk to Albert Fish who runs the aquarium and who looks quite like a turbot himself. He waives the fifty-pence entrance fee for me, because I come in so often to have a look at the mermaid's purse and the cuckoo wrasse and the lobsters. I'm not allowed to hold anything in the touch pool any more after I held a starfish too tight and hurt it, but sometimes Albert lets me help him feed the conger eels. Feeding the eels is my favourite part. We throw in a couple of salmon heads and the eels go absolutely crazy. You have to be careful not to hold onto the salmon head for too long, though, because the eels will take your hand off if you let them. Albert says that the last person who ran the aquarium lost two fingers feeding the eels, and now the eels have a taste for human blood.

Mostly I just stay in Fowey, wandering about, listening in case anything exciting has happened. Sometimes you might hear some gossip about Robert Hoolhouse and his wife, or the plan for a new hotel up by Gribbin Head, but it can be hard to hear – people whisper all this because they think William Podmore might be listening too. Once the shops start shutting and the street lamps turn on, I make my way back to the hotel where I eat dinner by myself in the hotel dining room.

The hotel never has anyone glamorous staying at it. There is a smarter place nearby with a swimming pool, so the only people who stay at The Cliff Hotel are quiet old men and couples who don't talk to each other over dinner. Last year there was a couple that spent the whole time in absolute silence, until the final day when they sat on different tables. This year the man came back with a thin redhead with a high-pitched laugh and too much lipstick.

The only person who lives here full-time is Jean Lee, whose feet are too swollen for her to walk, so she sits on a chair in the lobby all day telling Aunt Maria that she is filing things wrong and that the windows need cleaning. Jean Lee must be nearly eighty now, but she is as sharp as a little paring knife. Nothing passes Jean. Her beady, black eyes see into every corner, watching out in case someone in the dining room holds their knife the wrong way or an ornament has a speck of dust on it. She yells from her chair, barking orders at the maids and telling Aunt Maria she has put on weight, even though Aunt Maria is paper-thin – even thinner than Mummy was. Aunt Maria is terrified of Jean, but since Jean is pretty much the hotel's only customer for most of the year Aunt Maria has to put up with her. For the past few months, Jean has had a companion living with her: Dorothea Waddington. Dorothea is about thirty and looks like a handkerchief that someone has blown too many times – all crumpled and limp. Dorothea bears Jean's needling and cruel jokes awfully patiently. She just smiles and sighs, drooping a little closer to the floor every time. I wouldn't be surprised if Dorothea turned round one day and just pushed Jean down the stairs. I wouldn't tell on her if she did.

The hotel chef, Joseph Vacher, is French and he lives in the hotel too. He has worked here for years, even though he only meant to stay for a summer. He is as round and oily as a doughnut, with toasted brown cheeks from standing over the oven. Joseph smokes all day and the ash goes into all the white sauces and gravy, but he lets me eat the leftover puddings off people's old plates, so we get on just fine. Last year I went into the kitchen to see if there was any spare sticky toffee pudding and I found him hunched on the floor, crying and moaning in French. When I asked him what was wrong he wouldn't tell me. I think it's because he wanted to work at The Ritz in London, and The Cliff Hotel is certainly not The Ritz in London.

Once dinner is finished, I'll wander around the hotel a bit, maybe let myself into some of the rooms and turn some of the pictures the wrong way round, or, if we have guests who are out to dinner, I'll go into their room and have a snoop around their things. One couple brought a dirty mag with them, and another man had a bag full of stuff he'd nicked from the hotel: forks and napkins and a small decorative swan from the lobby mantelpiece. One of the things I like most is putting on their make-up. Some women come with bags of the stuff – bright-red lipstick and blue eyeshadow and coral blusher – so I'll slather it all on in their bathroom and then scuttle back to my room to examine myself in the mirror. My face looks better with make-up on, especially when I paint the eyeshadow all the way up to my eyebrows and put on lashings of lipstick, but if Uncle Frederick catches me with a painted face then I'll get a smacked bottom or worse, and have to take it all off with Joseph the chef's kitchen scrubber, so I have to be careful not to get caught. I'll dash back to my room, hiding behind the ferns as I go, and then I'll look in the mirror and practise crying for a bit, letting all the eyeliner drip down my face in curdled black streaks.

Before I go to bed I write in my diary, or I might write a story. I've written a lot of stories about Jean falling out of the window and getting smashed up on the rocks below, and stories about getting magical powers and being able to turn the whole estuary to ice. Mr West's favourite story that I wrote last term was called 'The Sailor's Last Wish', and it was about a sailor who found a genie trapped inside his wooden leg, but he fell in love with her, so he wouldn't let her out by making a wish. It was quite good, but it was only two pages long and I got a bit bored after the sailor cut off the genie's arms. I've been thinking that maybe I should write a story about my summer in Fowey.

I've been reading a book called *The Murderers' Who's Who*, which I took from Granny's bookcase before I left. It has a bloody dagger on the cover, and an alphabetical list of all the best murderers from the past. It even has some pictures in the middle, mostly of the victims, which you can look at to get a bit of an idea of what all the murderers have done. So I'll read that in bed, waiting for the sun to come up.

I don't sleep very well. I never have. When I was little it was because Malcolm wouldn't let me, crouching over me as I slept with his backwards head whispering in my ears. Then Mummy and Daddy died and I couldn't stop thinking about them getting all wozzled up in the ship propellers, and now not-sleeping is just a habit. So I'll not-sleep all night, until Aunt Maria comes and knocks on my door with her feathery knock and tells me I have to get up. Sometimes I'm so tired I can barely move or think straight. But it gets better after I've had a couple of strong coffees from the buffet. Jean doesn't approve of twelve-year-old girls drinking coffee, but truly, Jean can get fucked.

3

Something in the Water

'Peculiar' is one of my least favourite words. Everyone is always describing me as 'peculiar', especially grown-ups. They called me peculiar when I gave the school gardener lemonade with wee in it, and they called me peculiar when I went to school wearing one of Granny's suits. Grown-ups never understand any of my jokes, but then kids don't really either.

Something peculiar did happen this week, though, and there's no other word for it.

I was up by the castle ruins throwing stones at some seagulls when I noticed a boat in the sea below. It was a fishing boat and the men on it were wearing bright-yellow coats and trying to pull up a torn, green net.

They were yelling at each other, but not in an angry way. Their voices were high and a bit scared, like when Mummy yelled at Daddy and he would say, 'You're hysterical, darling.' Hysterical. That's what it sounded like. So I edged forward as far as I could over the parapet, making sure not to lean too far and go tumbling off the cliff. The men struggled with the net, and I thought for a minute they might have caught a shark or a dolphin, but then they hoisted it up a bit more and I saw what it was that they had been screeching about.

It was a lady. Bluey-white and all tangled up in the net, with seaweed coming out of her mouth. She definitely wasn't a mermaid, because she was naked and she had two legs, even though one of them looked like something had had a good old nibble on it. The fishermen hauled her out of the water and she slid onto the deck like a fish. She was fat as a seal, with orange hair, bright against her blue body.

I ran back down to the town so fast that I tripped on some loose stones and skimmed the skin right off my knee. But I didn't have time to stop because I knew that any minute the body would be in the harbour, and I really wanted to get a closer look.

By the time I got to the quay, there was already a group of jabbering tourists peering out at the boat. The town's weedy policeman, PC Ted Nodder, tried to shoo them away, but they wouldn't budge. One man even had his bird-watching binoculars out and was excitedly describing what was taking place while his wife shrieked, 'Oh DON'T, Paul! I can't BEAR it!' as she grabbed for the binoculars to get a better look.

The boat chugged towards us, and PC Nodder looked as though he might have to be sick into his hat. The fishermen had done their best to cover up the body with their yellow coats, but we could still see a marbled hand poking out and some wet, rusty hair filled with sand. The tourists gasped, rooted to the spot – they weren't going to miss this for the world, and neither was I. I followed in PC Nodder's wake as he made his way to the front of the crowd. He tried to clamber onto the boat and got caught out with one foot on the quay and one on the deck, until the fishermen eventually had to haul him aboard. I giggled, and a tourist in culottes glared in my direction.

PC Nodder peered under the fishermen's coats, looking a bit queasy. Even though he was trying to look official we could all see how wet with sweat his face was. 'Right,' he said to the fishermen, 'we need to get her onto the quay.'

The fishermen glanced at each other. 'Are you sure, sir?' the bearded one said. 'She's not really in a fit state to be moved.'

PC Nodder looked at the crowd of people who had gathered to watch.

'Of course I'm sure,' he said crossly, loud enough that we could all hear him clearly. 'Let's give the girl some dignity. We can't leave her under a pile of coats all day. And the ambulance will be here soon – they'll need to be able to get to her.'

'Yes, sir, but –'

'Don't argue, please,' PC Nodder snapped. 'Just help me move her.'

It soon became apparent why the fishermen had been so reluctant. The body was like a chicken leg that had been stewed too long; every time one of the men tried to pick her up, a piece of sodden flesh slid off the bone. PC Nodder shrieked as a handful of thigh came off in his hand.

'WHAT THE HELL ARE YOU DOING?'

The voice came from a tall man pushing through the crowd. We all turned to look, and saw that it was Dr Thomas Cream, the town GP.

'Ted,' Dr Cream said to the policeman, 'you do realise that you cannot move this body, don't you?'

'It's PC Nodder, thank you,' Ted snapped. 'And I can do whatever I please. I'm the one in charge here.'

Dr Cream sighed patiently. 'Yes, I see that. But if you continue to move this body then it'll be hardly more than a skeleton by the time it gets onto the quay. I think you've already noticed that the flesh is quite soft.'

'Yes, I had noticed actually, thank you,' PC Nodder muttered, wiping his hands on his trousers.

'Good, then why don't we wait until the ambulance comes with a stretcher? And in the meantime you can clear the quay of people so that the ambulance can get through.'

'YES, I KNOW WHAT TO DO THANK YOU, DR CREAM!' PC Nodder huffed, wobbling off the boat onto the quay.

The fishermen looked relieved, but the rest of us were furious – we all wanted to have a good old looky-loo, but Dr Cream was going to have us all cleared out. Paul with the binoculars looked even more put out than I felt.

As PC Nodder started moving people along, I slipped into the aquarium and pretended to look at the sea snails until I could see that everyone had gone, PC Nodder had hopped back onto the boat and it was safe for me to go back outside again.

It took a long time for the ambulance to come, but I stayed, and sat on a bollard and waited. I'm good at waiting. PC Nodder kept yelling at me to go home, but it's a free country. I'm allowed to sit on a bollard if I want to, and besides, he was too busy on the boat, peering under the pile of coats and holding his nose, to worry about me.

Finally the ambulance trundled down to the quay. Its siren wasn't on – no point, seeing as the woman was about as dead as you can get. Two men in green boiler suits jumped out of the ambulance with the stretcher.

The ambulance men tried to replace the coats with their sheet without revealing too much of the body, but with the rocking from all the people on the boat it was impossible, so in the end they just whipped off the coats completely and covered the body as quickly as they could. They weren't quick enough for me, though.

I craned forward to see and realised that the woman wasn't actually fat, but being in the water for so long had made her swell up like a sponge. Patches of her skin had gone, and the colour had rubbed off her, so she was as white as a marshmallow and threaded through with blue like a Stilton cheese. Her long fingernails were still painted red, even if some of them were missing. I could see from the flash I glimpsed of her face that her eyes had gone too and a few of her teeth. I wondered if there was a fish at the bottom of the sea, choking on a molar.

I read in one of my murder books that if you leave bodies long enough then they fill up with goo and go bang like balloons if you prick them. I could see the barnacled anchor near the dead lady's leg and was hoping that one of the ambulance men would tip her onto it by mistake and she'd explode all over the deck, but they managed to slither her onto the stretcher without so much as a pop.

I looked up and noticed that every window nearby was filled with faces, watching as the stretcher was hauled onto the quay. PC Nodder must have been aware of all the eyes blinking at him too, because as the ambulance men began moving the stretcher off the boat, he decided to try to help, but he stumbled and knocked the stretcher sideways onto the hard tarmac of the quay.

As it hit, the woman's mouth cracked open and something rolled out of it towards me. I knelt down and snatched it up. I didn't want to attract attention by looking at it, so I snuck it into my pocket as PC Nodder finished shouting at everybody to hurry up, as if the hold-up hadn't been his fault all along, and the fishermen and the ambulance men manically tried to scoop the woman back onto the stretcher.

It was then that George Brain stumbled into the quay. He was holding his wooden box, but even he could see that there wouldn't be much use in making a speech with all of this going on in the background. He stood gazing at the scene as PC Nodder opened the ambulance doors to put the body inside.

George Brain made his unsteady way over to my bollard.

'What's all this?' he asked, his breath stinking.

'They found a body in the water,' I replied.

'A body?' he said, as though I'd just told him the weather forecast. 'What sort of a body?'

'A woman. Red hair.'

'A woman in the water,' George Brain nodded. 'That sounds about right.'

'Are you going to do a speech about it?' I asked, looking at his box.

He watched as the ambulance began to drive away.

'Can't do another speech about it,' he sighed. 'Can't always be doing speeches about women in the water. The water's full of women.'

Before I could ask him what he meant, PC Nodder was standing over us. He told George Brain to piss off before he arrested him for being drunk and disorderly. George Brain just shrugged and walked off.

'Good luck with all them dead bodies,' he shouted over his shoulder as he departed.

'There's only one body, Mr Brain!' PC Nodder yelled back, but George Brain had disappeared into the pub.

PC Nodder turned on me. 'And what about

you, eh?' he said. 'What do you think you've been doing all this time looking at a dead body? It's not right, it's not . . . respectful. It's not the sort of thing little girls should be looking at.'

I wanted to tell him that from the look on his face earlier I had a better stomach for dead bodies than he did, but he carried on.

'Where are your parents? I've a right mind to tell them what their daughter's been up to all afternoon.'

Then I got to watch his wispy moustache droop with embarrassment while I told him in detail about my parents drowning and getting minced up in the ship's propeller. I even teared up a bit for good measure, to really butter the bread nice and thick.

'Right,' he spluttered. 'Gosh. I see, well then . . .'

After that he obviously felt guilty – he was really nice to me and insisted on giving me a lift back up to The Cliff Hotel in his police car. As we were turning up the hill I heard all the other policemen discussing the drowning over his radio. He looked at me nervously and turned it off.

My aunt was very upset when PC Nodder told her where I'd been. I pretended to be traumatised and shivered a lot, so she gave me a few cups of very sweet tea in the pink parlour, which is painted the colour of strawberry sherbet and is full of the Fair Maiden figurines that Aunt Maria collects. It's also where Jean sits and torments Dorothea in the afternoons.

Jean's black eyes glittered when she found out what had happened in the town. When Aunt Maria left to tell my uncle, Jean squeaked along the pink leather sofa towards me and started to probe me about the body. She wanted to know what it looked like, and who I thought it belonged to. Jean never likes it when something has happened in the town that she doesn't know about – it drives her mad, so I deliberately didn't answer her, pretending that I couldn't remember.

'Leave the poor girl alone,' Dorothea said, nervously blinking behind her smudgy glasses. 'She doesn't want to talk about it.'

Jean ignored her.

'Did it pong?' Jean asked, licking her lips. 'I bet it ponged to high heaven, left in the water like that.'

'Jean!' Dorothea gasped. 'Don't!'

'Oh, don't be so wet, Dorothea,' Jean snapped.

Jean leaned closer to me and clasped my arm with her bony fingers. She smelled of Parma Violets. 'Come on, child,' she said. 'You must remember!'

'Well,' I said, thinking I had better give Jean something to stop her going on, 'she didn't have any eyes left.'

Jean leaned back into the sofa to digest this, like a snake that had just swallowed a rat. 'No eyes,' she breathed. Dorothea shivered.

'Well, of course, it will be someone up at the caravan park that did it. I've always thought they should never have built that caravan park,' Jean tutted.

'We don't know that she was . . .' – Dorothea dropped her voice – '. . . murdered. She might have slipped on the rocks, or fallen out of a boat. She could have jumped, poor soul.'

'Well, I suppose that's true,' Jean conceded, annoyed. 'We'll have to see, won't we?'

Dorothea gave me a watery smile. 'Are you all right?' she whispered. 'I expect you'll have nightmares tonight, poor thing.'

'I never have nightmares,' I replied, because it's true. I don't have dreams at all.

4

Murder

The hotel was in chaos that evening. I hid behind one of the ferns in the lobby and watched my aunt fending off questions from the guests. The news of the dead lady had obviously made its way up the hill and people were worried. Aunt Maria isn't very good with people. I've never really understood why she works on the reception desk because she gets flustered and upset if anyone makes a complaint. She looked even more out of her depth than usual, white-lipped and hair frazzling out of its scrunchie, and when one guest demanded to speak to someone 'more competent' she burst into tears and Uncle Frederick had to come out of his study and take over. As he strode over to reception Uncle Frederick spotted me crouched in my hiding place and yelled at me in front of Winnie Judd, who helps out in the evenings.

I hate Winnie. Hate her. And she hates me right back. She is twenty-five but looks ten years older, because she wears too much make-up caked over her spots and dyes her hair an awful yellowy, crunchy blonde. She never does any work if no one is watching. I once spent a night secretly following her around the hotel, and the moment my aunt or uncle are out of a room she slips off her pumps and picks her toenails. She has a high voice and was once the Carnival Queen and never lets anyone forget it. I wouldn't be surprised if she sleeps in her dried-up old flower crown. Last summer some jewellery went missing from one of the hotel bedrooms and I copped the blame for it, even though I know for certain it was Winnie.

Winnie wears piles of gold bracelets that make her skin turn green at the wrists, and there's no way she would have passed up an opportunity to add to her collection. I tried to explain that to Aunt Maria, but she called me a liar and tried to make me write a letter of apology to Winnie. I refused and got in a lot of trouble with Uncle Frederick.

Winnie was watching while Uncle Frederick yelled at me in the lobby and she had this horrible smirk on her pearly-pink lips. I wanted to run over to her and pull out all her yellow hair, but I am nearly thirteen now and almost a grown-up, so I just went up to my room and pulled some of the stuffing out of the sofa instead.

Sometimes, when I'm angry, I get the feeling that I'm filled with conger eels like the tank in the aquarium, all cold and slithery. I once ordered some squid-ink spaghetti in a posh restaurant that my parents took me to, and when I looked down at the plate, all inky and sticky and knotty, I got the feeling that was what you'd see if you peeled back my skin: ribbons of black spaghetti all coiled up behind my ribcage. When I tried to explain this to Mummy, she rolled her eyes and said that I got it from my father's side of the family.

I used to get angry at school – red-faced, Uncle Frederick angry – and I'd have to go and sit by myself next door until I'd calmed down. But now I'm better at hiding it, keeping the eels nice and calm while I stick a pencil nib into my hand.

While I pulled the stuffing out of the sofa, I looked out of the window at the lights over the black water and wondered how long the body had been floating around inside it, brushing up against the underbellies of the boats.

It was only then that I remembered the thing that had fallen out of the woman's mouth, and I fished it out of my pocket and examined it. It was a small stone, slightly ridged, like one of the fossils that get washed up on the beach. I'd hoped it would be a clue. It might have had the murderer's initials or a pagan symbol carved into it, or a blood spatter on it full of DNA, but it held about as many murder clues as one of the pebble sweets I buy from Mr Queen.

Joseph the chef was below my window, smoking a cigarette and picking his nose, so I called down to him to save me some profiteroles from dinner because I was hungry and no one had given me any food, but he just sighed one of his big, French sighs and flicked his cigarette over the cliff. I always wonder why Joseph stays at the hotel. He doesn't like Uncle Frederick at all and is the only person who ever stands up to him. Sometimes I hear them having blazing rows in the kitchen. Once, when Uncle Frederick had really frightened Aunt Maria, Joseph threatened to hit him over the head with one of his saucepans. Uncle Frederick has sacked Joseph more times than I can count, but he always gives him his job back, because Joseph makes the best toad-in-the-hole in the world, and Uncle Frederick only really likes toad-in-the-hole. My theory is that Joseph stays because he thinks he's protecting Aunt Maria, but if that's true then he's doing a pretty terrible job of it.

The next morning Uncle Frederick came into my room with some chocolate spread on toast and asked me if I was all right. He sometimes does this, even when he hasn't done something really bad. I almost prefer the punishments to the apologising. It confuses me and makes me think he's on my side. He apologised for getting so cross and said that he wouldn't do it again, because it was not good for the hotel's reputation to be seen yelling at a child, no matter how naughty that child had been. I didn't think I had been naughty in the slightest, but there is no stopping Uncle Frederick when he starts one of his speeches, so I just let him get on with it.

He said that the lady who died had once worked with Aunt Maria, which is why she was so upset about the murder. I immediately perked up: so it *was* a murder! Uncle Frederick backtracked – he obviously wasn't supposed to tell me – and tried to change the story, saying that he didn't mean a murder after all, only an accident. But it was too late, and once he'd realised that the idea of a murder hadn't frightened me in the least, he sighed and ruffled my hair a bit, gave me one of his horrible kisses and left.

The best thing about there being a murder in Fowey is that it means there is a murderer in Fowey. It could be anyone. I know from my murder books that it's always the quietest, smiliest, most helpful person who's been the murderer all along, which makes it tricky, because everyone in this town is quiet and smiley and helpful.

For the last few days I have had my ears pricked even more than usual in all the shops and in the streets, and I've been nicking the local paper from out of the bins because silly Aunt Maria says I am too young to read the news. The whole town is jabbering about the murder, everyone gathered around on the cobbles, heads together, whispering. They couldn't be more excited than if the Queen or Cliff Richard had come to visit.

A few journalists have come to the town, so everyone is on their best behaviour. All the women are wearing an extra coat of lipstick and the hairdresser's is full of people getting a blow-dry or a trim in case they're on the evening news. Suddenly everyone is the victim's best friend or confidante, even the people who only had their groceries scanned by her once, or saw her walking past in one of her short skirts.

While this frenzy of excitement has been going on, I've been watching to see if anyone seems suspicious and finding out as much about the dead woman as I possibly can.

These are the things I have learned:

1. The murdered woman was called Susan Newell. She was thirty-two and worked at the supermarket.
2. She was strangled.
3. According to the national paper that I pilfered from one of the guests' tables after breakfast, she had TWO boyfriends, but neither of them did it because they were both away. I thought that maybe they both did it together and gave each other alibis, but one was in Manchester and the other was in Cardiff, so that was a shame.
4. She was Fowey's Carnival Queen fifteen years ago, and the photograph that the papers keep using is one of her waving

from the top of her parade float with a terrible hairstyle and purple lipstick.

5. She went to live in London for a few years to try to be a singer, but came back to Fowey when that didn't work out. The Flower twins in the bookshop told me that she couldn't sing a note and that she was 'always a bit above herself, God rest her soul'.

6. Everyone keeps on saying 'God rest her soul' every time they talk about the dead woman, especially when they say something rude about her.

7. She was 'a bit of a trollop' (God rest her soul), according to something I overheard in a conversation.

8. The police are exploring 'every avenue'.

9. PC Nodder has no idea what he's doing.

10. They are sending some police from Portsmouth to come and help PC Nodder.

I asked Joseph what he thought about the murder while he was making crème brûlée and he told me that his cousin was in prison for murder in France. Apparently he hit his ex-wife with a car because she was trying to stop him from seeing their children. I thought that seemed like quite a good reason, and Joseph agreed with me. In France it is called a *crime passionnel* – a 'crime of passion' – and a lot of the time people get off for it. I'm not sure Susan Newell was killed in a *crime passionnel*, though. Fowey doesn't really seem the kind of place where people are passionate about anything, except for hydrangeas and sailing and keeping the cobblestones free from lichen and not getting into trouble with Mr Podmore.

I am absolutely determined to solve the murder. I have been compiling a little book of clues. I think I know more about murder than anyone else in this town (except for maybe the actual murderer). Whatever happens, I'll definitely be able to solve it before PC Nodder does. That man doesn't know his arse from his elbow. He couldn't find the murderer if he was strangling someone in front of him.

5

A Visitor

There is a boy in the hotel.

He arrived with his mother yesterday. He is about my age, I think, though he is a lot taller than me. He dresses like someone half our age, in Boy Scout shorts and pulled-up socks and an old-fashioned jumper, and has long blond hair.

His mother looks like a sofa cushion, completely round and stuffed into chintzy floral dresses, and she clucks around him, straightening his jumper and pushing his hair out of his eyes and speaking to him in an ickle-wickle baby voice. He stamped his foot in the lobby, because he wanted his own bedroom and not to sleep on a cot bed in his mother's room. The mother looked very tearful but eventually agreed – she seemed to be worried about him sleeping alone for the night, which seems pretty mad as he's nearly six foot tall. Jean said the boy seemed 'very spoiled indeed' and tutted a lot as the exchange went on, until the boy turned around and scowled at her, which made me immediately like him.

I tried to catch his eye in the dining room, but he completely ignored me.

This morning I found him kicking around in the pink parlour, looking at all the ornaments. His mother had clucked off to arrange a day trip to the Lost Gardens of Heligan. I brought out one of the papers I'd taken from the dining room and started reading it in an aloof way, until eventually he turned around to look at me.

'You've got weird hair,' he said finally. 'I thought you were a boy.'

'You can talk!' I said. 'You look like Goldilocks!'

He flinched; this was clearly a sore point.

'Mother won't let me cut it,' he said, kicking a decorative pouffe.

'Just cut it yourself, that's what I do!'

'She wouldn't like that.'

He looked around the room, taking in all the pink and the frilly curtains and the doilies.

'So you live here then?' he said. His voice was a lot deeper than most of the boys my age.

'Sort of,' I replied. 'I live here in the summer. My aunt and uncle run the hotel.'

He nodded.

'I'm an orphan,' I added, just to get things going a bit.

'I wish I was an orphan,' he said, squeezing a china pig tightly.

'My parents got chopped up by a ship propeller.'

'Cool.'

He came to sit on the sofa next to me and looked at the paper.

'Did you know her?' he asked, pointing at a picture of Susan Newell holding a glass of champagne and looking a bit squiffy.

'No, but my aunt did. Apparently she was a bit of a trollop, God rest her soul.'

He looked at the photo more closely.

'Who do you think killed her?' he asked.

'Well, it's usually a vengeful lover,' I replied. 'Or a pervert.'

His mother came in and looked at me disapprovingly.

'What are you looking at, lambykins?' she asked him. 'I hope you're not reading about that horrible *thing*.'

'No, Mother,' he said, his voice suddenly higher than it had been before she came in. 'We were looking at the cartoons in the back.'

She fanned her flushed face with relief.

'Oh goodness!' she breathed. 'Of course you were! Silly me! Come on, popkin, we're off to the gardens.'

He sighed and got up.

As they left, his mother turned and gave me a look of absolute poison. Really! It's not my fault if he's interested in the murder!

Later, at dinner, he came in and sat across from

me. He had changed into a jumper with little sailing boats all over it, with a frilled collar sticking out.

He picks his nails a lot. And I'm allowed to say that because I pick mine too, much to Granny's annoyance. He hardly has any nails at all, just a few moon shards surrounded by half-pulled ribbons of skin. We sat for a few minutes in complete silence while I ate my dinner and he ate his fingers.

Eventually I decided to be the bigger person and spoke up.

'How were the Lost Gardens?' I asked.

'Boring,' he said, peeling off a strip of cuticle.

'Didn't you see the Venus flytrap?' I asked.

'No.'

'If it's hungry they let you feed it with a bluebottle.'

'It eats the whole thing?' he asked, perking up a bit.

'Yup, the jaws just close on it and it swallows it down, wings and all!'

'Mother would never let me do anything like that. We just looked around the rose garden.'

'Where's your dad?' I asked.

'Don't have one,' he replied. 'He left before I was born, so Mother brought me up.'

'Did your mother make you that jumper?' I asked.

He glanced at it and nodded. 'She knitted it – it's a copy of one I had when I was little. She makes all my clothes. When I grow out of them she just makes them a size bigger, exactly the same.'

'Do they tease you about it at school? They tease me about my Vlad T-shirt.' I pulled up my jumper so he could see Mr West's T-shirt underneath.

'I don't go to school,' he said. 'I'm home-schooled.'

'But how do you make friends?' I asked.

'I don't really have any friends,' he replied, tugging at his fingers even harder.

'Me either. But I kind of hate everyone, so it doesn't really matter.'

He looked up at me and smiled for the first time. He has a gap in his teeth.

We talked for ages, as quietly as we could because we could see Jean tilting her head towards us from the lobby, straining to hear. She kept moving her chair closer and closer to the doorway so that she was practically in the room.

The boy's name is Miles Giffard. He is thirteen. He lives in Birmingham. He is an only child. He has a food phobia that means he can only eat dry food or ice cream. His mother is very rich (her father invented some kind of valve that goes on washing machines), but she doesn't like to spend the money, so they live in a two-bedroom bungalow. Miles used to sleep in a room with his mother, but this year she finally let him move next door, although she insists he keeps the door open so that she can check on him. I didn't tell Miles how creepy this arrangement is, because I didn't want to hurt his feelings.

Miles is also obsessed with true crime. It turns out we have read a lot of the same books on it, and both his and my favourite picture is the one of Mary Kelly with her face torn off and her guts hanging out in the Jack the Ripper book.

I like him.

He is going to help me with the murder.

6

The Plot Thickens

The plot thickens.

That is all anyone around here keeps saying: 'The plot thickens.'

Another girl was fished out of the water at St Catherine's Point.

The town is absolutely hysterical with excitement, even though they're all pretending to be devastated and go about wearing black and crying a bit.

The Cliff Hotel is starting to fill up with people,

which Jean is furious about because it means that Aunt Maria has less time to listen to her complaints. The phone has been ringing non-stop and the reservations book is full of Aunt Maria's terrified scrawl.

Uncle Frederick is thrilled about this and is licking his big red lips. He has doubled the hotel's room rates. Jean sniffed about this and said she thought it was in bad taste, and even Dorothea seemed to agree with her, but Uncle Fred says it is simply 'making hay while the sun shines'. The journalists and photographers and rubberneckers and fancy policemen from Portsmouth have to stay somewhere, he says, so why shouldn't they pay for it?

Miles and I have been spending a lot of time in the pink parlour, listening to what all the new people have been saying, but it sounds as though the police don't have any idea – even the ones from Portsmouth, who you'd think would have their stuff together when it comes to this sort of thing. Portsmouth is a hotbed of crime according to Jean.

The second body belonged to a girl called Cordelia Botkin, who worked at Admiral Cod's fish and chip shop. I even met her a few times! She was pretty, with greasy hair and skin from all the frying. I remember her because she shook a load of extra vinegar onto my chips, even though Admiral Cod himself (Roy) told her that she wasn't allowed to give me any more. She winked at me and gave me a free sachet of ketchup too (usually 5p!). I was sorry when I heard it was her they found smashed up on the rocks at St Catherine's Point, especially when it could have been Winnie instead. Sometimes murderers just do not murder the right person, which is a shame, but I suppose they have to snatch away the first person coming down the alley. They can't really be picky about it.

According to a photographer who is staying at The Cliff (whom I have cleverly befriended in order to learn more about the murders), Cordelia Botkin didn't have a boyfriend at all, and there was no one the police could find who had a bad word to say about her. Obviously she was as nice to everyone else as she was to me, and gave everyone extra vinegar. So now they are starting to think what I could have told them AGES ago: we are dealing with a serial killer.

No one can believe that the murderer is a local, although I think they're kidding themselves here. So does Miles. Everyone keeps saying that it must be someone travelling through the town, someone up in one of the caravan parks or hiding in the woods. The Flower twins say they can hear someone walking over the cobblestones in the middle of the night, but they've been too afraid to peep through the curtains to see who it is. I said I thought it was probably one of the policemen – they now guard the town at night – but the Flowers said the footsteps did not have a 'policeman's gait', whatever that means.

Everyone is very worried about what Mr Podmore will think about all this. It doesn't really matter what colour the bunting is or that all the windowsills are painted the exact same daffodil yellow when your perfect town is now on the map for a couple of grisly murders. No one has heard a word from Podmore yet; they haven't even had one of his letters. I expect he's just sticking it out in Podmore Hall, probably hoping the whole thing will just go away.

It's pretty unlikely that it will, though. Cordelia's picture is on the front page of every newspaper in the country. It's a much nicer photograph than Susan Newell's – it's a picture of Cordelia graduating from university, holding a rolled-up diploma, so the whole nation has taken her to their hearts far more than they did poor old Susan Newell with her glass of wine and cleavage.

Cordelia was found with a sea-urchin fossil in her mouth. When I found this out I rushed up to my room and got the stone out of its hiding place to have another look at it. I held it up close to the light: it looked like a sea urchin fossil all right! Which means it is almost definitely the murderer's calling card. If I know anything about murderers it's that they LOVE leaving calling cards, it's just in their nature.

Miles is obsessed with the stone; he spends hours rolling it between his palms. I wondered whether I should give the stone to the police, since it's probably a clue, but Miles said they are useless and would only lose it anyway, so we should keep it safe. Miles sleeps with it under his pillow every night so that no one finds it. He doesn't sleep well either.

As soon as Cordelia Bodkin's body was found, Miles's mother wanted to cut their holiday short and go back to the safety of their bungalow, but Miles got very angry and refused to leave. He told her she was being silly because it wasn't young boys or old mums getting dredged out of the sea, so he was safe. Since Miles gets whatever he wants, eventually she agreed to stay. Jean teases Miles's mother mercilessly, and calls her Mrs Tiggy-Winkle behind her back and talks loudly about the murders around her because she knows it upsets her.

Jean's favourite new tactic is to talk about Miles's hair and how it makes him look like a young woman, and how if she were Miles's mother she would be worried that the murderer would mistake him for one and strangle him in the woods. The first time she said this Miles's mother burst into tears, and Uncle Frederick had to give Jean a quiet ticking-off.

Mrs Tiggy-Winkle doesn't like me any more than she likes Jean, and stares daggers at me when I try to invite Miles to sit with me at breakfast or go exploring with me in the town. Miles told me she thinks I'm 'bad news', which has really given me a spring in my step.

Last night Mayor Hoolhouse held a candlelit vigil on the quay for the murdered women. The whole town was there, including everyone from the hotel. Uncle Frederick and Joseph the chef had to carry Jean down in her chair from the lobby, while Dorothea fussed beside them, worrying that Jean might be tipped out. I prayed that she would be, but she clung on tight with her withered little claws and stayed put all the way down.

The Mayor had on all his robes and his big clanky necklace and was very solemn and gave a very long speech about how proud he was of the town for sticking together in such grave circumstances. You couldn't see for all the photographers' flashes, and the Mayor's wife made a big show of dabbing her eyes with a silk hanky. PC Nodder stood awkwardly beside her, patting her until she shrugged him off with a twitch of her velvet shoulder.

All of the grief-thieves (which is what I heard one of the journalists call them) – mostly women from the Yacht Club and a few tourists who had been swept up in the excitement – muscled their way to the front of the vigil to blink moistly so they made sure they got in the papers, while Roy from the Admiral Cod wept into a commemorative parcel of chips. His wife looked a bit cross about this and kept on hissing at him to pull himself together.

Cordelia Botkin's family just stood quietly to one side, her father holding up her mother, and her younger brother holding so hard onto a bunch of flowers that they had begun to bruise.

I don't know where Susan Newell's family were. Maybe they couldn't face it.

During the minute's silence Miles and I played a game to see how long we could hold our hands over the candle flame before pulling it away. I could only do it for a few seconds, but Miles could do it for ages without even wincing. I don't think he can feel pain at all.

Miles and I peeled off away from the crowd before the end of the vigil. Our idea was to stand on the wall on the street further up so that we could get a good look at everyone as they were leaving. This was Miles's idea: he thought we might be able to spot a guilty face and wanted me to point out who everyone was.

As we walked round the back of the Town Hall, we heard some sobbing echoing from inside the disused public toilets. I didn't want to go in, because the lights were turned off, but Miles called me a bed-wetter and a weed.

'Why don't *you* go in then, if you're so brave?' I whispered.

'Because it's the ladies' toilet,' he replied.

I thought this was neither here nor there since the toilets didn't even work any more, but I didn't really want to argue and look like a coward.

The toilets were dark, except for a little orange light from the lamppost shining in through the small window. I could see the cubicles in front of me, all closed. The weeping was coming from behind the last door.

'Hello?' I said.

The weeping stopped.

'These toilets don't work any more,' I said.

The weeper sniffed.

There was a little rustling from behind the door, and I nearly scarpered.

'There aren't any tissues or anything,' I said, 'if you came here to blow your nose.'

The door unlocked, and I took a step closer to the exit. It was all very well for Miles to send me in for investigative purposes, but I didn't fancy getting murdered in a disused toilet like an idiot.

A figure stepped out of the loo, and once the orange light hit his face I could see it was Peter Queen, from the sweetshop.

'Oh, it's you,' he said, wiping his eyes with his sleeve. 'I should have known.'

'I just came in to see if you were all right.'

'I bet you did,' he said with a laugh. 'You always like to know what's going on in this town, don't you? Sticking your nose in.'

I ignored this. It's not my fault if I like to know things.

'What are you doing in here?' I asked.

He sighed and leaned up against the sinks.

'All this . . . the vigil. Brings it all back.'

'Brings what all back?'

He twisted the tap back and forth; no water came out.

'My wife,' he said, his voice a bit wobbly. 'She drowned too. They found her up the river. Fifteen years ago now. Feels like it happened this afternoon.'

'Was she murdered too?' I asked.

'You like to cut to the quick, don't you?' he said, shaking his head. 'No, she wasn't murdered. Just unlucky. Took a tumble while she was walking the dog.'

'What kind of dog was it?'

Mr Queen looked at me as though this was the maddest question he'd ever heard.

'It was a Jack Russell. Jinx. I had to have him put down. Couldn't look at him.'

'That doesn't seem very fair,' I said. 'It wasn't the dog's fault your wife drowned, was it?'

Mr Queen changed the subject. 'Who's that lad you've been skipping around with? Tall boy, long hair,' he asked.

'That's Miles,' I replied. 'He's staying up at the hotel for the summer.'

'Is he your boyfriend?'

I was glad it was dark enough that he couldn't see me blush. Thank goodness Miles wasn't there to hear it.

'No!' I said, so loudly that it echoed round the toilet.

'All right, only asking,' he said. 'It's nice for you to have a friend. It's not right, you always on your own every summer.'

'I suppose not.'

Mr Queen wiped his eyes with his jumper.

'Why don't you pop round for tea sometime?' he said. 'Above the shop.'

'Are you a pervert?' I asked.

Mr Queen got a bit upset about this question, but it seemed like a good idea to check with a murderer on the loose, so I don't know why he took it so personally.

'No! It's just . . . it's nice to talk to someone, that's all,' he explained. 'You can bring your friend if you like.'

'All right,' I said. 'I should probably go now. My uncle and aunt will wonder where I am.'

Mr Queen nodded.

I left the toilets just as the vigil was winding down. Someone was singing 'Somewhere Over the Rainbow' along to an acoustic guitar; some of the crowd were joining in. As Miles and I left to find our wall, we heard Mr Queen start sobbing again. Honestly! It was fifteen years ago! He shouldn't be so upset about it now. Miles agrees, and says that it isn't really very manly going around crying in ladies' toilets.

7

Rubberneckers

The murder fanatics are all here now. They've turned up in their droves from all over the country with their glasses, their greasy hair and their note pads. Miles and I have been sneering at them. I don't know why they think they can solve the murders when we've been trying for ages and haven't found a single useful clue.

The hotel is so full of people that some of the rubberneckers have to share rooms. I snuck into one the other night, and they had a wall full of photographs and maps. It didn't seem like they'd got very far, since most of the clues were cut out from the papers. But I swapped a few of the photos around and turned a map upside down just in case they were getting somewhere.

A new policeman has arrived on the scene all the way from London! His name is DCI Arthur Rottman, and he wears an enormous pair of mirrored sunglasses and has been going around asking questions, PC Nodder snapping crossly at his heels. Miles and I hid behind one of the bookcases in Flowers' Bookshop this afternoon, while DCI Rottman questioned the twins. He was quite strict, and got the twins all in a tizzy asking for alibis and how well they'd known the victims. PC Nodder kept on interrupting, telling Rottman that he'd already asked these questions and it was no good going around upsetting everyone. DCI Rottman told PC Nodder to go and stand outside.

Once Nodder was gone, Rottman turned up the heat on the twins. I could tell Miles was enjoying it because he was gripping onto my arm very tightly, peeping between some second-hand copies of *Alice's Adventures in Wonderland*.

Rottman said he was convinced that people in the town knew more than they were letting on, and he went and sat behind the twins' desk, putting his feet up. Classic power play.

Margaret and Phillipa didn't know what to do and started gabbling all at once about the strange men up in the caravan park and the Second World War pillboxes in the woods where the army snipers used to sit that sometimes had tramps living in them. Rottman didn't seem interested in either of these things, waving his hand impatiently.

'You two have got to suspect someone,' he said in a quiet, insinuating way. 'You must know all the comings and goings round here. Who do you think it is?'

'No one from this town!' said Margaret (or Phillipa). 'Never someone from this town!'

'Not even, let's say, George Brain?' Rottman asked, waggling his eyebrows.

The twins looked at one another nervously.

'George Brain isn't quite right,' said Phillipa

(or Margaret). 'He's not been right ever since the mine closed. He likes to drink and get on his soapbox, but he'd never do something like this. We've known him since he was a child!'

Rottman flicked through his pad, licking his thumbs as he went.

'I have someone here telling me that when he is on his soapbox Mr Brain likes to say there are girls in the water. Mermaids. You don't think that sounds rather incriminating?'

'Mermaids? Well, that just goes to show, doesn't it? He's not in his right mind,' said Phillipa/Margaret.

'But he threatened that there would be more girls in the water, you don't dispute this?'

'But there *were* girls in the water!' said one of the twins. The other one elbowed her in the ribs.

Rottman sat up in his chair.

'What do you mean?'

The twins blinked back at him.

'You'd better tell me,' he said threateningly.

'We live by the water,' said one of the twins quietly. 'We're a seaside town. Of course over the years there have been . . . drownings.'

'Even in Daphne du Maurier's day,' the other twin nodded. 'She even wrote about it in one of her stories – girls being pulled out of the water. It was set in Venice, but . . . well, she lived here, didn't she, Mr Rottman?'

'*DCI* Rottman, thank you,' he said sharply. 'I'm not interested in what some lady novelist from years ago had to say on the matter.'

The twins bristled. Their beloved Miss du Maurier being reduced to a mere lady novelist was more than they could take.

'If that's all, *Mr* Rottman,' one said sharply. 'We have to be getting on with our day.'

Rottman bared his teeth in a sort of weird grin. 'All right then, ladies,' he said, getting up. 'Thank you for your time.'

He left the shop with a swagger, PC Nodder tripping to catch up with him outside.

'What an unpleasant man,' one twin said.

'Very unpleasant indeed,' agreed the other. 'He won't get very far bullying us all. I wonder what Mr Podmore would think!'

'Mr Podmore would be very displeased. Very displeased indeed.'

It has been burning hot for the last couple of days. Miles still has to wear his scratchy jumpers that his mother knits, even though it makes him short-tempered and sweaty round the temples. People just stand on their doorsteps in the town, fanning themselves, watching out for any news on the murders. The quay is starting to stink with fish. Now that Rottman is here, there seems to be a bit of fever in the air, all prickly and sweaty. I think everyone is nervous that he's going to dredge up all their old secrets.

Aunt Maria is frantic with worry that people are too hot in the hotel and has made Uncle Frederick drive to the garden centre to buy all the fans. Uncle Frederick was furious about it and shouted at Aunt Maria in the lobby for being such a fusspot, his eyes goggling. He usually only frightens her in their private flat in the hotel, so Jean was tickled pink to see a bit of a show. I think the heat and the murders have got to him like they've got to everyone else.

Joseph the chef is very tearful, especially since all of his puddings keep melting in the heat. He says he came to Fowey to get away from things like this. I told him, no offence, but I didn't think the murderer was after a fat Frenchman, so he was perfectly safe, but this only made him sadder.

Miles and I have been making hundreds of lists. Lists about the murder suspects mostly, but our main interest is who is next. We spend a lot of time getting into the murderer's mindset, stalking about the town looking at all the girls, thinking about which ones we'd like to kill most. I've given my murderer a limp, and drag my foot behind me in order to feel more murderous. Miles doesn't like the limp; he thinks it's silly. He prefers a more methodical route. He looks at all the girls and divides them into categories: age, prettiness, hair colour, clothes, jobs. Sometimes, he asks me to go over to one of them and ask a few questions so that he can find out whether they have a boyfriend or not. He says they're more likely to speak to a girl. So I sidle up to them and butter them up a bit, while Miles scribbles away in the shadows.

So far, the main potential victims are:

1. Belle Gunness. Twenty-eight. Pretty.
   Dark hair. Works in the bank. Wears long
   swooshy skirts and smokes clove cigarettes.
   No boyfriend.
2. Cathy (don't know last name). Nineteenish.
   Very pretty. Blonde hair. Gap-year student.
   Boyfriend works at the Flagon pub.
   Eyebrow ring.
3. Christina Edmunds. Thirties. Quite pretty.
   Curly brown hair. Married to Mr Edmunds,
   who runs the Yacht Club. Sad eyes. Posh.

We think that any murderer worth his salt would
choose one of these three. I thought it might be a
good idea to warn them that the murderer might
be onto them, but Miles thinks we should wait
and see what happens.

Mrs Tiggy-Winkle doesn't know about any of
this. She thinks we spend the day climbing trees
and examining ruins. If she knew how interested
Miles was in all the gory stuff, she'd take him out

of Fowey lickety-split, so we have to make up all the things we've done, and hide our research up our shirts. She spends the evening fussing over him and smoothing down his long hair. Aunt Maria and Uncle Frederick never ask where I've been. I don't think they could care less if I was the next body washed up on the rocks.

Winnie Judd is enjoying the attention of all the reporters no end. She's got herself on the news twice, her chest heaving as she remembers her dear friends and reminds everyone that, like Susan Newell, she too was once a Carnival Queen. I wish someone would murder her.

This evening I saw Winnie kissing her boyfriend in the hotel car park when she should have been working. They were all sweaty up against the bins by the kitchen. Her pink uniform around her waist and lipstick all over his face.

She spotted me and went absolutely crazy, calling me a dirty peeper and a nosy little bitch as she tried to pull her skirt back down.

I told her that I couldn't care less about her kissing her gross, spotty boyfriend and it was

ee country and I should be allowed to stand
y the bins if I wanted to. I said I would tell
Uncle Frederick on her for skiving off work and
for calling me a little bitch. That shut her up.
She was seething but she knew I had won, so
she just stormed off, with her boyfriend sloping
along behind her wiping the lipstick off his face.
I shouted after them that they should be a bit
more careful with a murderer knocking about.
She gave me the finger as she kicked the kitchen
door open.

When I told Miles this he nearly died laughing.
He wanted to know all about the kissing, and
what else I thought they might have been doing.
I told him about Winnie's skirt and he didn't
believe me, so he made me describe it a few more
times. I added in a few details to give the whole
thing a bit of pizzazz, and Miles found it all very
intriguing.

I was going to tell Aunt Maria about Winnie
too, to get her sacked once and for all, but Miles
made me promise not to. He says that other
people's secrets are like shiny pound coins, and

that we should always save them up for when we need them. Personally I'd rather watch Winnie get sacked now, but Miles begged and eventually I got bored and agreed.

He is right, though. It feels nice hanging onto secrets. I feel like my satchel is filling up with them – Winnie's and mine and the murderer's, all clammed up together next to my sweets in the dark.

8

The Murder Games

Miles and I had a picnic this afternoon. We went
up to the ruins and laid down a tablecloth that
we'd filched from the dining room. Joseph had
made up some fish paste sandwiches for us but
they were too wet for Miles's food phobia so we
chucked them at the seagulls and ate my pebble
sweets instead.

It's nice to have a friend who isn't a grown-up
like Mr West or invisible like Malcolm. Mummy
and Daddy were always cross that I didn't have

any friends. Like it was my fault! They were always inviting their friends' children over for tea, but they never liked any of my games and always asked to leave early. Miles loves my games.

Lately Miles and I have been playing a new game.

In the game we go for a walk, usually up round the cliffs, the parts where the ramblers don't go, and then suddenly Miles will run up ahead and hide, and I have to walk by myself, looking frightened (sometimes I even do feel a bit frightened, because I don't know when Miles is going to appear). Then, when I least expect it, Miles will leap out from his hiding place and drag me somewhere, and I have to kick and scream as though he is the murderer and I am his victim. I do a lot of wriggling and say things like, 'Pleeeease, mister, don't hurt me! I'll do anything you ask!' – like the actresses do in horror films. When Miles has me in his hiding place he wrestles me to the ground and pretends to strangle me, mostly with his hands, but once he took off his scratchy jumper and did it with that. The strangling usually takes about five minutes, depending on how dramatic my death is, and by the end of it we're quite sweaty and I'm covered in dirt from the floor. Sometimes, mid-strangle, I look up at Miles, and his face is all murderous and red, so I get the giggles, but Miles does not like that at all and then he really does strangle me a bit, until I stop.

After the game this afternoon I asked Miles a bit more about his life. He twisted off a piece of grass and started tearing it up. He had wet grazes all over his knees from kneeling over me during the game.

'I don't know,' he shrugged. 'It's fine.'

'But wouldn't you like to go to school?' I asked.

'I used to. But I learn more at home than I ever could at school. I'm reading Nabokov. Have you ever read Nabokov?'

'Yes,' I lied.

Miles rolled his eyes at me.

'But don't you get bored at home with your mother fussing over you all day?'

Miles thought for a minute.

'Sometimes,' he admitted. 'Especially when she makes me pluck her eyebrows for her, and things like that.'

'Gross!' I said.

'But it's not that bad mostly. She lets me do whatever I like, and cooks me all my favourite things and buys me anything I want.'

'Like what?'

'Like books and games and stuff.'

'That's okay I guess,' I admitted. Granny has never bought me anything, except for my school uniform.

Miles leaned closer to me.

'Once,' he whispered, 'I wanted a dog. So Mother went down to the pet shop and bought me a puppy. But it was really annoying and peed everywhere and you had to walk it four times a day otherwise it yapped all the time. I said she should take it back to the shop, but the shopkeeper wouldn't let her return it.'

'So what happened?'

Miles shrugged.

'Mother drowned it.'

'What?' I said. I couldn't imagine Mother Tiggy-Winkle drowning a puppy.

'She took it to the pond in our garden and held it underwater for five minutes. Just shoved it in there and held it down. She lied to me about it and said the shop had agreed to take it back after all, but I saw her do it from my window,' he said.

'Were you sad?' I asked.

'A bit, maybe. I don't know. I don't really get sad about things,' he said.

I nodded. I knew exactly what he meant.

'Maybe your mother is the murderer,' I said.

Miles laughed.

'Maybe. Along with your auntie,' he replied.

'No one would ever suspect them – it would be the perfect crime,' I said.

'Mother is killing off everyone in the world so I never leave her,' he laughed. 'Watch out, you'll be next.'

I thought a bit about asking the next question, and decided to go for it.

'Have you ever had a girlfriend?' I asked.

Miles gave me a look like I'd asked the stupidest question in the world.

'No. Not allowed.'

I didn't ask him the question after that, because I was too embarrassed. But sometimes I catch Miles looking at me in a way that puts the eels back in my stomach, but this time they're all warm when they're slithering around in my guts. I nicked some eyeshadow from the chemist and have started wearing it, but it doesn't look like Miles has noticed yet.

'So what's this book you're reading about then?' I asked to fill the silence.

'Oh, just a girl,' he said. 'The cover has a painting of her sitting with her leg up, so you can see her knickers.'

I don't think he's read the book at all. He's just looked at the cover and is showing off about it, but I don't mind. I show off too sometimes.

When we got back down to the town there was a big hoo-ha going on in Ship Street. Rottman had been trying to question George Brain and George was having none of it. A little crowd had gathered to watch as Rottman tried to calm George Brain down. PC Nodder looked on smugly as Rottman struggled to keep it together.

'Mr Brain,' Rottman said, 'please will you keep your voice down? There's no need for a scene.'

George Brain took a wobbly step towards Rottman, who turned his face away from the stinking breath.

'I've been telling you!' George Brain said, a bit tearfully. 'I've been trying to tell everyone. There are spirits inside the cliffs, waiting to snatch us all away.'

'Enough of this superstitious nonsense, please, Mr Brain!' said Rottman.

'It's not superstition! I've said for years, haven't I?' George Brain looked desperately around at the crowd. Peter Queen was peeping out from his sweetshop. George Brain caught his eye and pointed at him.

'Your wife, Peter!' George Brain yelped. 'The spirits took her too!'

Mr Queen pulled back into his shop and closed the door.

The crowd was starting to turn on George Brain – they started jeering and telling him to shut up and to leave poor Mr Queen out of it.

'If you go on distressing everyone, I'll be forced to take you into custody,' Rottman threatened.

At the back of the crowd, I noticed Cordelia Botkin's father. He wasn't joining in with the jeers, just looking sadly at Mr Brain.

'We've angered the spirits,' Mr Brain continued. 'They've got it in for us. We mined the cliffs too deep and now they're after us all.'

Cordelia Botkin's father burst into tears.

'Right,' Rottman shouted. 'That's it! Come with me, please, Mr Brain. Can't go around distressing the deceased's family.'

'You were asking me!' George said, stung by the injustice of it.

'You just keep your mouth shut,' Rottman said.

'But he's right!' Cordelia Botkin's father said.

The crowd was silenced.

'I took the shoes away,' he whispered.

'I'm sorry?' Rottman said, letting go of George Brain's arm.

'The lucky shoes. We were renovating – I threw them away,' Mr Botkin sobbed.

Rottman looked baffled. So did Miles. But everyone else knew what he meant.

Suddenly Mayor Hoolhouse was on the scene, his wife clutching his arm.

'What on earth is going on here?' he demanded. He looked at Cordelia's crying father, and then at Rottman.

'Inspector,' Mayor Hoolhouse seethed, 'if you cannot conduct your investigations with any decorum then may I at least ask you to hold them privately? I think this town has been through enough, don't you?'

PC Nodder flushed with pleasure. 'That's the problem with these city policemen,' he whispered loudly. 'Don't have any manners.'

Rottman glared at PC Nodder and then at Mayor Hoolhouse. He took a deep breath. 'I am merely trying to discover what has happened here,' he said.

'Well, could you please find out more quietly?' the Mayor said.

The crowd giggled.

Rottman nodded coldly. He looked at George Brain, who looked like he might chuck up at any moment.

'I'm not finished with you yet,' Rottman hissed.

Back in the hotel garden, we sat on a table at the bottom of the steep iron steps that lead up to the hotel. This was where Jean used to sit before her feet got too bad for her to sit outside. She'd drink her afternoon bottle of wine and yell at anyone who didn't take the stairs slowly enough, shouting, 'You'll break your neck!' at Aunt Maria as she walked down carefully with a tray.

Miles asked me about the shoes.

'It's a local thing,' I said. 'All the houses in the town have children's shoes in the walls from hundreds of years ago. There are some in the museum. They're supposed to ward off bad spirits and keep the house safe. Sounds like Cordelia's dad chucked the lucky shoes out when he was doing up their house.'

'Oops,' Miles said.

'Yeah. No wonder he feels so bad.'

'You don't believe in all that stuff, do you? Only babies believe in that stuff,' Miles said.

'Course not!' I replied.

So what if I do believe in it? I thought. But I didn't want Miles to think I was a baby.

Winnie came down to the garden to clear away the tea things and glared at us.

'Get off that table,' she snapped. 'Those tables are for guests only.'

'I'm a guest,' Miles said, pulling his door card out of his pocket.

I gave Winnie a nice big wide smile.

'Could I have a glass of tap water, please?' Miles asked Winnie.

'I have to go all the way up to the kitchen to get it,' Winnie sulked. 'I've got to clear away all these teas.'

'Great,' Miles said. 'Thanks.'

Winnie turned on her heel with her hands clenched.

Miles is amazing.

9

Go Fish

There is a mangy cat that keeps showing up at the hotel. It's missing an eye, and it stinks. Aunt Maria has taken a shine to it and has insisted that she and Uncle Frederick take it in. She thinks the hotel could to with 'some character'. I personally think that a whiffy one-eyed cat isn't the kind of character a posh hotel should be striving for, but Jean and Dorothea were watching, so Uncle Frederick agreed through gritted teeth. Miles is even more annoyed than

I am because he is allergic to cats – they make his eyes go puffy.

Aunt Maria has named the cat Ruffles. Miles and I have named it Fucko.

Uncle Frederick doesn't come and visit me at night nearly as much as he used to. I think he's worried about all the police being around. I haven't told Miles that about Uncle Frederick yet. Even though Miles is my best friend, he still might not understand.

Mrs Tiggy-Winkle is even more nervous about Miles than usual, so we have to be doubly careful.

It's my birthday soon. My aunt and uncle haven't mentioned it. Normally Joseph makes me a cupcake and puts a little candle in it, but I haven't heard him talking about it, so I wonder if everyone has forgotten.

I told Miles about it being my birthday soon while we were sitting in his room playing Go Fish.

'Mother goes mad when it's my birthday,' Miles said. 'Last year she got me a huge cake shaped like a dinosaur, and a magician.'

'That sounds a bit babyish,' I said.

I wish someone had got me a dinosaur cake and a magician.

'The magician had this trick where he brought a huge snake out from inside his top hat. And he cut me in half, and made my mother disappear,' he said.

'Wasn't there anyone else at the party?' I asked.

Miles gets snappy when I ask questions like this.

'No, I told you, no one's allowed in the house except for us,' he said.

I shuffled my cards around a bit.

'Would you do that if you could?' I asked.

'Do what?'

'Make your mother disappear?'

Miles thought about this for a moment.

'Probably,' he grinned. 'And cut her in half first.'

'Then you wouldn't have to wear those silly clothes, and you could have friends over and no one could say anything about it,' I said.

'I wish!' he said. 'I'd just have to go and live in an orphanage, and that would be even worse.'

'Not if you didn't tell anyone,' I said. 'I could come and live with you, and we could look after ourselves.'

Miles thought about this for a bit. And then I started to feel silly.

'Only kidding,' I said. 'I wouldn't want to wash all your smelly clothes.'

Miles threw an ace of spades at me.

'So what do you want for your birthday then?' he asked.

'I dunno,' I said. No one had really asked me this question since Mummy and Daddy died, so I couldn't think. 'Maybe a new notebook? Mine's nearly full.'

'Bo-ring,' Miles said. 'I'll get you something way better than that.'

Miles's mother stuck her head around the door.

'What are you two up to?' she said, looking at me accusingly.

'Nothing, Mother,' Miles replied.

'Well, you know that we've booked to go to the restaurant on the coast for lunch, chop-chop. Get your coat on,' she said, clapping her hands.

'It's boiling outside,' Miles said.

'It won't be all afternoon,' she said. 'It'll get breezy and then you'll catch a cold. And you look so sweet in your little blue coat.'

Miles got up and started to put on his coat. I hung around, hoping his mother might invite me to lunch. She looked at me impatiently.

'Why don't you go and play with someone else for a change?' she said. 'Miles is on holiday with me, you know – we can't have you taking up all his time.'

I looked at Miles, hoping he would stick up for me or demand I come to lunch with them. But he didn't.

I spent the afternoon by myself in the Seagull Tea Rooms and had two hot chocolates: one with dark chocolate and then a white chocolate one for pudding. The lady who runs it is called Mrs Hindlay. Her husband left her a few years ago, and she has a teenage son who occasionally does the washing-up and picks the spots on his chin. I think she is quite bored, because she spent a lot of time trying to peer at my notebook and asking me what I was writing about. I told her I was writing a story about murder and she told me that it absolutely wasn't an appropriate subject for a girl my age and that I should be more respectful because there were actual murders going on. She was really getting into the swing of a lecture about children being children and violence on the telly and how someone should be looking after me and how you wouldn't find her son Ryan writing bloodthirsty stories at my age. So I told her that her precious son once showed me his willy round the back of the aquarium, and that shut her right up.

Peter Queen in the sweetshop looked even more misty-eyed than usual and barely looked up from the manky old photo of his wife when I went into his shop. I was trying to buy a bag of cinder toffee to take with me to the quay and he dreamily looked up at me and asked about Miles.

'Nice for you to have a friend,' he said. 'I always thought you should have a friend. You've always been running around by yourself. No one should be alone for the summer, not at your age.'

'You said that before,' I said.

'It's not nice to be on your own. I know that better than anyone.'

He looked at me in the way that grown-ups sometimes do when they remember I'm an orphan. All pitying and sad. Never mind that I get on perfectly well by myself. Grown-ups always think that when you're young you can't handle anything. But it's grown-ups who can't look after themselves. Look at Mr Queen, still blubbing over his wife who died a million years ago, or Aunt Maria who spends all day shivering with terror, or George Brain who is so drunk he can't stand up, or stupid Mr Podmore who never leaves his own house. Miles and I are the only people in this town keeping it together, but grown-ups think we're incapable of looking after ourselves because we're younger than them.

It makes me hate Mr Queen for being so soft, but I don't show it. I do what I always do when grown-ups talk to me like that, which is look really wistful and sad until they bugger off.

'Have the toffees on me,' he said.

I left.

'And don't forget about our tea!' he called after me. 'Anytime you like! Bring Miles.'

I didn't really feel like thinking about Miles. Especially since he had just betrayed me. I thought about leaving one of his murder notebooks on his mother's bed for when they got back from their swanky lunch. Then she'd take him away and it would serve him right.

This is the problem with friends. You think they're all right and then they just stab you between the shoulder blades. There's no point in having friends at all, really. Or family. Your family will just die anyway. It's better to be alone, really, and not to like anyone.

I was starting to get the eels feeling again. Cold and dark. I shoved some of the cinder toffee into my mouth, enough to give me a proper sugar rush, and sat on a bollard watching the boats, wishing one would hit a rock so that there would be something exciting to watch.

I noticed one of the reporters doing his rounds down the shops, trying to ask people questions.

Everyone has started clamming up around here now. Jean told me that the whole town got a letter from Mr Podmore, telling them that their hysterical behaviour on the news was not befitting of the town, and that under no circumstances should they speak to the press.

Well, I didn't get a letter from Mr Podmore, and even if I did I couldn't care less what he thinks. So I ran up to the reporter as he was coming out of the bakery. He looked younger than the rest of them and quite nervous, and seemed pathetically grateful when I said he could interview me if he liked because I knew everything there was to know about Fowey.

I told him lots of things about the town, and he scribbled them down, trying to catch up with all my news. I told him that Mayor Hoolhouse wore a wig, and that the eels in the aquarium had a taste for human flesh, and that Mr Podmore refused to leave his house. I added a few things that I'd heard about people having affairs, and then made some stuff up for good measure, just to add a bit of colour to my story. I was telling him that we always sacrifice a cow at the end of Regatta Week when he stopped writing and looked at me.

'Are you making all this up?' he said.

'No,' I replied innocently.

He shoved his pad back into his pocket and looked quite cross.

'This bloody town,' he said. 'You're all nuts.'

He walked off without saying thank you.

Back at the hotel, Jean was needling Dorothea in the pink parlour. Dorothea had asked for a night off to go to the pub quiz.

'I don't know why you want to do that, Dorothea,' Jean sniffed. 'Who'd want you on their team? You don't know anything! You'd just embarrass yourself.'

'I could just listen then,' Dorothea said quietly. 'Listen to the questions.'

'Doesn't sound very fun to me,' Jean said. 'Sitting by yourself, listening to the quiz. People would find it odd. They'd laugh at you.'

Dorothea looked down at her lap.

'And, really, I didn't want to bring this up, but you've forced it out of me,' Jean continued. 'Walking around the town in the dark isn't a terribly clever idea, is it? With all of these killings going on.'

'Please, Jean,' Dorothea said, squeezing her eyes shut. 'You know I don't like talking about that.'

'Well, you might not like talking about it, my girl, but you'd happily stroll around by yourself at night. It's practically asking for it, if you ask me. It's almost like you want to get murdered, Dorothea.'

'Jean, please . . .'

'And I'd be the one who'd have to identify your body in the morgue, wouldn't I? No thought for me or my delicate sensibilities . . .'

'I won't go,' Dorothea said.

Jean settled back in her chair happily.

'Quite right, Dorothea, quite right. You're not as silly as you look.'

Miles and his mother hadn't yet come back from the restaurant. My angry feelings from earlier had gone away a bit, and I was glad I hadn't tried to get him in trouble. But I was starting to feel something worse – I was starting to feel worried and upset that he wouldn't come back. That his mother had taken him back home and I wouldn't see him again.

I looked at the cherub clock: it was nearly seven.

I felt the prickly feeling in my nose that I hadn't had since I was little. I didn't want to cry in front of Jean, so I ran up to my room before anyone noticed.

Miles was in my room.

'What are you crying about?' he said.

I was so happy I couldn't think of anything to say for a moment.

'I stubbed my toe,' I said, sniffing back the tears.

'Oh right,' Miles said.

He pulled something out from his pocket and handed it to me.

It was something wrapped in a napkin, a smear of brown.

'What is this?' I asked, thinking it must be a joke.

'Chocolate cake,' he answered, not looking me in the eye. 'I saved some for you from the restaurant while Mother was in the bathroom.'

I didn't know how to answer. It was the nicest thing anyone had ever done for me.

'Thanks, I'll eat it later,' I said.

The chocolate cake is under my pillow, still wrapped in the napkin. I'm never going to eat it. I'm going to save it forever.

10

The Muffin Man

Uncle Frederick used to tell me a story called 'The Muffin Man'.

The Muffin Man lived in the woods, up by Boddick Brook. He had a pitted, flat nose, which is why everyone called him that. He was a rag-and-bone man, which meant he found old rubbish from the scrapyard and sold it door to door. The Muffin Man gave his customers an option: they could give him money or food for the scraps they wanted, or they could tell him a story about their lives. No one ever chose to give the funny old man money or food, they always told him a story, even as he got thinner and thinner as the years went on.

Over the years the Muffin Man got to know everyone in the town from the stories they told. He got to know the people who were happy, because they told him stories about swimming when they were children, and he got to know the people who were bitter and unkind, because they told him rude stories about their neighbours. One day, the Muffin Man disappeared, leaving his rusty rag-and-bone cart in the wood, but he had written down all the stories, every single one, over the years, and pinned them up all over town, so that there were no secrets any more.

The whole town descended into fighting and tears, because everyone suddenly knew everyone else's business, and all of their nasty gossip and secrets and desires were out in the open. And the Muffin Man watched from a hiding place, laughing at everyone, because they had thought that their stories were cheaper than a slice of cake or a penny.

My uncle told me that the moral of this story was never to talk. Never to tell anyone about private things that happen in the dark, even if someone like the Muffin Man offers you something for it, because private things, they have a way of making their way into the light.

Someone is always listening in this town, even if it isn't the Muffin Man – it might be Mr Podmore, or one of the police, or even me.

Uncle Frederick said that if you listened closely at night you could hear his cart rattling along the cobblestones. I used to be frightened of the Muffin Man.

11

Tea at the Sweetshop

I took Miles to the aquarium to meet the eels.
Albert Fish had promised not to feed them until
I brought Miles in, but when we got there Albert
was just rinsing out the orange chum bucket.

When I gave him a look, he sighed.

'Can't leave the eels hungry just for you,'
he said.

I don't think he realised how much I had been
talking about it to Miles.

'Can I stick my hand in?' Miles asked.

Albert looked down into the eel tank, where they were all sitting at the bottom, digesting their lunch.

'Can't let you do that, I'm afraid,' Albert replied. 'I'd get into trouble.'

'But they're full, aren't they?' Miles said. 'They won't bite me if they're full.'

I gave my most pleading eyes to Albert, but he ignored them.

'Sorry,' Albert said. 'You can stroke one of the starfish in the touch pool if you like.'

I thought this was a bit rich, since I wasn't allowed anywhere near the touch pool, and Albert didn't know Miles from Adam. But Miles wasn't interested in the touch pool.

Albert showed Miles around the aquarium, explaining about all the fish and how long they'd been there, and which ones could get on with others. There was one angry catfish that wouldn't share a tank because he'd bite the other fish.

Albert tapped the catfish's tank as he circled around his orange castle alone, his whiskers sagging. 'You're a naughty one, aren't you?'

'Maybe the others weren't nice to him,' I said. 'Maybe that's why he bit them.'

'There's no excuse for biting,' Albert said. 'If you're a biter you have to go in a tank by yourself, that's the rule.'

Miles asked about the mural on the wall, a seascape full of shoals of fish and waving seaweed, which was peeling and bubbling after years in the damp aquarium.

As Albert talked enthusiastically about the artist – a long-dead woman who had been quite a famous painter in her day – Miles leaned up against the conger eel tank, his hands behind his back.

Albert was too excited about pointing out the lady's signature up the side of a painted seahorse to notice Miles's fingers slip into the tank.

I watched as the conger eels stirred, aware of something in the tank with them. Miles's fingers were dead-white waving in the water against the blue light of the tank. I wanted to shout at him to stop, but Albert hadn't noticed and I didn't want to get Miles into trouble.

One of the eels started to slither up through the tank towards Miles's hand. It opened its jaws. Needle teeth stuck out of its grey gums in pointed clusters – they'd strip the skin off in chunks. Miles continued to nod at Albert, calm, his hand in the tank, the eel darting closer to him.

I held my breath.

The eel looked at Miles's fingers, sizing them up with its stony eyes. It twitched. There were scars on its lips.

Swim away, I thought. Swim back down to the bottom. Don't take his hand off. His mother will take him away and I'll never see him again.

The eel nudged Miles's hand with its head, once, then twice, testing to see what it was. I waited for the flash of teeth, hardly able to look. It didn't come. The eel lost interest, nudging once more and then curling away.

As it brushed past, Miles stroked its back with his finger.

Albert turned to point at an old photograph of the aquarium, and Miles lifted his hand out of the tank and wiped it on his jumper. He glanced over at me and smiled, just as the eels nestled back in their rocks at the bottom of the tank.

On our way to meet Peter Queen for tea at the sweetshop, I asked Miles what the eel had felt like.

'Nice,' he replied. 'And cold.'

Peter Queen's flat was small and in the eaves above his shop. Miles had to stoop a bit to avoid hitting his head on the beams. Mr Queen seemed nervous – he ushered us into his sitting room, wiping sweat from his forehead. He had combed his red hair into a wonky side parting and was wearing quite a smart waistcoat covered in moons and stars and a knitted tie.

The sitting room was tiny, with barely enough room for all of us to sit in it. Miles and I perched on his sofa while Mr Queen shakily brought in a tray with the tea things. He had put out a little bowl filled with my favourite sweets, and I helped myself to a handful while I looked around the room, trying not to catch Miles's eye in case we got the giggles.

Every surface of the room was crammed with photographs of Mrs Queen, Peter's wife. But once you looked closely you realised they were all the same photograph. Mrs Queen was standing in front of a grey wall wearing her wedding dress, with her lace veil blowing around her face. She was smiling, slightly gap-toothed, and looked barely older than a teenager – you could see a rash of spots under the heavy wedding make-up. The photo had been printed over and over, in different sizes, in different frames. Some of the copies were in black and white or sepia for variety.

Above the fireplace was an oil painting, copied from the photograph, that didn't look quite like Mrs Queen. The painter clearly hadn't got the hang of the teeth – the smile looked all gummy and wrong. On the sofa, there was the same picture, in needlepoint this time, and a throw with her name on it: Chrissie.

'I see you've noticed my dear wife,' Mr Queen said, handing a cup to Miles.

Mr Queen took one of the photographs and looked at it longingly.

'We weren't married long,' Mr Queen sighed. 'It was only a few weeks before she was taken from me. I only have the one photograph.'

Miles looked up at the oil painting.

'Ah yes!' Mr Queen said. 'I painted that myself. I wanted to add a few horses in the background – she loved horses – but I couldn't do the legs properly.'

You could just see the shadow where a horse with wonky legs had been painted over behind Mrs Queen's head.

'I think it's brilliant,' I said, because I didn't want to hurt his feelings. Miles snorted a bit and covered it with a cough.

'Thank you,' Mr Queen said. 'I'm no artist, really, but I thought it would be a fitting tribute.'

'Did you not have any photos of both of you?' I asked. 'On your wedding day?'

Mr Queen began to pour out the tea into little gold teacups.

'No,' he said. 'Chrissie didn't think I was very photogenic.'

I looked at Mr Queen and had to admit

that Chrissie had a point. With his ratty teeth and sticky-outy ears he wasn't going to win a modelling competition anytime soon, but it did seem a bit mean of her not to let him be in his own wedding photographs.

'I'm glad now,' Mr Queen said. 'I wouldn't want to sit in here looking at photos of my ugly mug all day.'

Miles picked up the needlepoint cushion.

'Did you make this too?' he asked.

'Oh dear, no!' Mr Queen scoffed. 'I'm not one for needlepoint. I commissioned it from the knitting shop. I don't think they quite got Chrissie's essence, do you? But there's only so much you can do with wool, I suppose.'

The knitting shop had given Chrissie angel wings and had embroidered the date of her death on a scroll below her face.

'Do you think she was murdered?' Miles asked suddenly, adding three sugars to his tea.

Mr Queen cleared his throat awkwardly.

'No,' he said. 'She just slipped on the path. Some people just slip like that.'

I could tell that Miles wasn't convinced, but he sipped his tea and didn't push it.

'Who do you think the murderer is?' I asked. 'Jean at the hotel thinks it's someone from the caravan park.'

'I don't know who it is,' Mr Queen said. 'But I'm sure they'll find them soon.'

He picked up the teapot again.

'More tea? I've got some Welsh cakes downstairs if anyone would like one.'

'The police aren't much good, are they?' Miles said. 'You'd have thought they'd know who it is by now. If they're not careful there'll be another body soon.'

'Miles and I know all about serial killers,' I added. 'Once they get a taste for it, it's only a matter of time until they do it again.'

'Well, I'm sure the police are doing their job,' Mr Queen said. 'How are things up at The Cliff?'

'All right,' I said. 'It's full of people. Aunt Maria gets a bit overwhelmed.'

'A bit!' Miles scoffed.

'I'm sure she's doing her best,' Mr Queen said.

'Uncle Frederick is thrilled about the murders,' I said. '"More money in the till," he always says.'

Mr Queen took a prim little sip of his tea. 'I'm sure he's not really thrilled,' he said.

We sat quietly for a bit. There isn't much to talk about to grown-ups.

'They found a dead body at my school once,' I said to fill in the silence. 'A woman had a heart attack up by the playing fields.'

'How terrible,' Mr Queen murmured.

'She was quite old.' I shrugged. 'And we all got the day off so the police could take her away.'

Mr Queen looked a bit queasy and changed the subject again.

'How are you enjoying your holidays, Miles?' he asked. 'You're not bored in our little town?'

I waited nervously. My great fear is that Miles is bored.

'It's been all right,' Miles said.

I was so relieved I felt all silly and giggled a bit into my tea.

'I wish I could be your age again,' Mr Queen said. 'Everything gets worse as you get on. Your wife dies. All your friends move away.'

'You could get a new wife,' I said helpfully. 'You have a sweetshop. Girls love sweets!'

'I don't want a new wife!' Mr Queen shouted, thumping his fist on the arm of his chair. One of the nearby pictures of Mrs Queen toppled over.

Miles and I stared at the floor, a bit embarrassed, while Mr Queen twitched in the corner, trying to calm down.

'I wish you'd stop going on about all this,' he said, sweat gathering above his lip. 'I don't want to talk about my wife.'

'Then maybe you shouldn't have her picture up everywhere then,' Miles said.

'But I don't want to forget her,' Mr Queen said miserably.

Make your mind up! I thought. But instead I asked if he had any Turkish delight.

'No,' Mr Queen said. 'I'm out of Turkish delight.'

We all looked at our tea for a bit. Mr Queen's eyes had gone all sad and misty again.

'Well,' he said in a fake-jolly voice, 'I'd better get back downstairs. Can't have the sweetshop closed while I chatter away to you all afternoon.'

He began to gather up the tea things noisily.

'But we only just got here!' I said.

'I'm sorry,' Mr Queen said. 'It was a mistake to invite you both here. You don't want to talk to me. No one wants to talk to me. You should be outside playing . . . or whatever it is you both do.'

'We do want to talk to you!' I said. 'Don't we, Miles?'

Miles shrugged.

'We do!' I continued. 'We want to talk to you about the murders. We're trying to find out what everyone thinks.'

Mr Queen crashed the tea tray down on the coffee table.

'That's it!' he said. 'You shouldn't be so obsessed by these murders. It's not right. It's . . . it's macabre.'

'Everyone else is interested in them,' Miles pointed out. 'It's not just us.'

He'd got Mr Queen there.

'Still, it's not the sort of thing children should be thinking about,' Mr Queen said.

It was clear Mr Queen wasn't going to change his mind, so we got up. I poured a few of the sweets into my satchel.

As we left we passed a card table. On it was an enormous jigsaw, with thousands of pieces. It was the same picture of Mrs Queen that was all over the room. It was almost complete, but it was missing two pieces.

Mr Queen saw me looking at it.

'Her eyes,' he said. 'I can't find her eyes.'

12

Jean

When we got back to the hotel, Mrs Tiggy-Winkle was livid. She was pacing up and down the lobby, while Jean watched with a sly smile on her face. Winnie was pretending to polish the stair rods, chewing gum and listening in.

'Oh here they are!' Jean said. 'They haven't been murdered after all!'

Mrs Tiggy-Winkle rushed up to Miles and gave him a great big bosomy hug.

'Where were you?' she asked. 'We were

supposed to go for a coastal walk this afternoon!'

'No, Mother,' Miles said. 'I went to the sweetshop for tea. Don't you remember? I told you about it yesterday.'

'No, I do not remember!' she said. 'I've been sick with worry. Thank goodness Jean was here to support me.'

Jean rearranged herself smugly in her chair. I knew exactly what sort of support Jean had been offering, needling away, winding Mrs Tiggy-Winkle up into a frenzy.

'I've given you too much freedom,' Mrs Tiggy-Winkle said. 'You and this little miss here.'

She nodded savagely in my direction.

'This was supposed to be our special holiday! Just us!' she said. 'And you leave me all on my own, day in, day out.'

She looked as though she might burst into tears. Winnie watched with her mouth hanging open, polishing forgotten.

'Sorry, Mother,' Miles said.

'Don't you want to spend time with me?'

Mrs Tiggy-Winkle wheedled, batting her eyelids at her son.

'Yes,' he said.

'Good!' she said. 'Well, you're to start behaving like a good son from now on, and to stop wandering off with *her* the moment my back is turned.'

I waited for Miles to contradict her, but he just kicked at the floor. 'Yes, Mother,' he said.

Mrs Tiggy-Winkle beamed with pleasure.

'There's a good little popkin!' Mrs Tiggy-Winkle said in her baby voice. 'Now, up you pop to change for dinner. I've laid clothes out on your bed for you.'

Miles didn't look at me. He just shoved his hands in his pockets and walked up the stairs.

Mrs Tiggy-Winkle turned on me, her fingernails suddenly in my arm. Jean craned forward and licked her lips. Winnie was breathless with excitement.

'Now, listen here,' she said – her breath smelled of humbugs. 'You just leave Miles alone. I know what grubby-minded girls like you want. Don't think I don't see the way you trail after him.'

I struggled to pull my arm away but she gripped even harder, pushing her face close to mine.

'He's very handsome, I know that! I'm not blind!' she continued. 'I know what you're after. But he's not like that. He's a little boy! And this is our holiday – our special holiday together! So you just leave him alone!'

She was red in the face now, her breath coming in gulps. She let go of me.

'I've tried to be pleasant,' she said steadily, 'but really, it's too much!'

'Well, maybe he doesn't want to spend time with you,' I said. 'Maybe he wants to spend time with someone his own age for once! Not cooped up with you all day.'

Her eyes narrowed and she looked me up and down, trying to intimidate me.

'We'll see who he wants to spend his time with,' she said, her voice all sickly-sweet.

She turned on her tiny trotters and sashayed up the stairs, stepping over a giggling Winnie. I couldn't move, couldn't think through the fury.

Once Mrs Tiggy-Winkle had disappeared, Jean raised her eyebrows.

'My, my!' she said.

'FUCK OFF, JEAN!' I shouted.

Winnie gasped.

'I'll tell your uncle you said that!' Winnie said, delighted.

'Go on then!' I shouted. 'See if I care!'

'Filthy,' Jean said, shaking her head. 'Filthy, filthy.'

Aunt Maria stuck her head in nervously from the parlour.

'Is everything all right?' she asked. 'I heard shouting.'

Winnie flipped her hair and told Aunt Maria that I had said 'the f-word' to Jean. Aunt Maria looked like she might faint.

'Fetch Dorothea, would you?' Jean said, wobbling her voice dramatically. 'I don't feel well.'

Aunt Maria trembled. 'Of course,' she whispered. 'I'm so sorry.'

She dipped back into the parlour to fetch Dorothea.

'I expect to have some remuneration,' Jean called after her. 'For my trauma. That is, if I survive the night.'

Jean's eyes glinted at me.

Aunt Maria returned with a fussing Dorothea.

'You should tell Mr Manning,' Winnie told Aunt Maria smugly. 'He'll want to know what's gone on.'

Aunt Maria winced. 'Well, I'm not sure . . .' she said.

I wanted to beg her not to tell Uncle Frederick. I'd have got on my knees if we were on our own together. But I couldn't bear to beg in front of Winnie and Jean.

'I'll tell him if you like!' Winnie said, grinning. 'He's in his office.'

'No, no,' Aunt Maria said. 'Thank you, Winnie. I can do it.'

When Aunt Maria gets really nervous or upset, she starts blinking like there's sand in her eye. She blinked over at me.

'I think you should apologise to Jean,' she said quietly.

I'd rather have taken the old-fashioned telephone from the side table and hit Jean in the face with it.

Jean looked at me, barely hiding her glee. Dorothea and Aunt Maria made pleading faces. Winnie laughed behind her hand.

I hate apologising, but there wasn't really much I could do.

'Sorry, Jean,' I said.

Aunt Maria and Dorothea let out their breath.

'I should think so too,' Jean sniffed. 'Using foul language to your elders.'

'She's apologised now, Jean,' Dorothea said.

'Not properly, she hasn't!' Jean replied, annoyed that Dorothea would dare contradict her. 'I'd have had my hide clean off if I'd ever uttered a profanity like that at her age! Rotten is what I call it.'

'She's only a child,' Dorothea said. 'Leave it now, Jean. I'm sure she didn't mean it.'

Jean glared at Dorothea.

'I wouldn't bet on it,' Winnie laughed. 'She's a spoiled little thing.'

Jean smiled her shrewd little smile at Winnie.

'Winnie, dear,' Jean said, 'why don't *you* take me up to my room.'

'But –' Dorothea said.

'You can stay down here, Dorothea,' Jean snapped. 'You can even go down to the pub. I know how much you've been longing to get away from me.'

Dorothea looked like an animal caught in a trap. She glanced at Aunt Maria, who looked away.

'Don't worry,' Winnie said, putting her arm out to take Jean's withered, grey hand. 'I'll look after Jean.'

The two women disappeared up to Jean's bedroom, leaving Dorothea fretting in the lobby.

'I shouldn't have said anything!' she cried. 'She'll be furious. I can't afford to be let go.'

Aunt Maria patted her shoulder. 'It'll pass,' she said. 'You know what Jean's like.'

I fiddled with my fingers, feeling like a bit of a spare part.

Once Dorothea had gone off to her room and Aunt Maria and I were alone in the lobby, I spoke.

'You aren't going to tell Uncle Frederick, are you?' I said, as quietly as I could in case he could hear in the study.

Aunt Maria blinked at me, even more terrified than usual.

'It doesn't matter if I tell him, does it?' she whispered. 'He'll find out. He always finds out.'

And he did.

Later, when all the guests had left the dining room, Uncle Frederick had a word with Aunt Maria.

I was outside, watching through the window.

Aunt Maria had made Uncle Frederick a cup of tea to calm him down. He slowly poured it all over the carpet.

I watched, holding my breath, as Aunt Maria got down on her knees and sucked up the spilled tea like a hoover, Uncle Frederick standing over her, making sure she got every drop, his foot on her back.

That's why you don't tell Uncle Frederick anything, even though he always finds out.

13

Night Visitor

I was reading *The Murderers' Who's Who* late that night when there was a knock at my door. I thought it was Uncle Frederick, coming to punish me for swearing at Jean. But Uncle Frederick has a door card and usually just lets himself in, so I tiptoed over to the door and looked through the peephole. It was Miles. I opened the door and he shot in, worried that someone might see him.

He was wearing some pyjamas – as childish as everything else he owns – which were covered in cartoon trains. He stood in the middle of the room, a bit restless, picking at his nails.

'I've stolen some cigarettes,' he said, pulling a blue packet out of his pocket. 'Someone left them in the parlour.'

I didn't know what to say. I felt a bit nervous.

'Shall we smoke one?' he asked. 'Out the window?'

'I don't really like the smell,' I said. The overflowing ashtrays in the kitchen were enough to put anyone off.

'Don't be a baby about it,' Miles said. He got a bit of a sneery look on his face whenever I didn't want to do something that he liked.

'I'm not being a baby!' I said. 'You're the one who won't even stand up to your mother! You're the baby.'

Miles lit the cigarette with some hotel matches. He didn't even cough. He looked out of the window for a bit, inhaling all the blue smoke silently, until I started to feel worried about mentioning his mother. Miles doesn't like being teased.

'I'm sorry about Mother,' he said. 'But she makes my life hell if I don't do what she says.'

'Don't be so stupid!' I said. 'You're just spoiled rotten!'

'You don't know what she's like,' he said.

I couldn't imagine Mrs Tiggy-Winkle doing anything but stuffing him full of cake and taking him to fancy restaurants and posh hotels.

'Sometimes,' Miles said, 'I wish she'd die.'

I didn't know what to say.

'Sometimes I think she could just fall down the stairs and break her neck, or get hit by a car. But she never does. She never goes anywhere and we live in a bungalow so . . . no stairs to fall down.'

'Then who would look after you?' I asked.

'No one,' he answered. 'You're all right, aren't you? You've got no parents.'

'Yes,' I agreed. 'But I have to live with my granny. And she's even more boring than my parents were.'

Miles tossed the cigarette out of the window.

'You know she makes me have baths with her,' he said. He didn't look at me.

I giggled.

'But how do you both fit in one bath?' I asked. 'You're so tall, and she's pretty big, your mum.'

'At home there's a big pink one,' he replied.

'But why?'

'She doesn't like being away from me. Even for a minute.'

I thought of telling him about Uncle Frederick and me, but pushed the idea away. It made me feel all wriggly and weird talking about Miles and his mum in the bath.

'I told Jean to fuck off this afternoon,' I said.

'What?' Miles said. 'Jean?'

I explained what had happened after Miles's mum had sent him off, and what I'd seen my uncle do in the dining room with the tea.

'Why'd he do that?' Miles asked.

'I don't know,' I said. 'He's like that. If I do something wrong, sometimes he punishes Aunt Maria for it. And if she does something wrong then . . .'

'He does something to you?' Miles said.

I didn't really want to answer.

'Can I have one of those cigarettes then?' I said.

Miles tossed the packet to me.

I didn't mind it, really, and I liked the way I looked waving it around, the smoke curling up to the ceiling. But it did make me feel a bit dozy and sick, with the taste of ash in my mouth and a numb patch on my tongue.

'We should get some drinks too,' Miles said, watching me smoke. 'Gin or something.'

'My uncle would kill us if he found out,' I said.

'Then we'll have to make sure he doesn't, won't we?' Miles grinned.

I don't think Miles really knows my uncle.

Miles opened the door to his mother's room. She was flung back on her bed, snoring, wearing a giant floral nightie, one fleshy arm draped over her face. The room smelled sour, like armpits and milk all mixed in with the strong rose smell of Mrs Tiggy-Winkle's perfume.

'What if she wakes up?' I whispered.

'She won't,' Miles said. 'She takes pills to get her to sleep.'

Miles pulled out a suitcase from underneath her bed – which, like everything she owned, was covered in a bright flower pattern – and rootled around in it. He pulled out an odd-looking wiggly bottle with a neon-green label saying 'Fowey's Finest' on it.

'What is it?' I asked.

'Dunno,' Miles shrugged. 'She collects the bottles. She bought it in the tourist shop. If we fill it with water, she'll never know.'

Mrs Tiggy-Winkle snorted and turned over in her sleep.

'Let's go!' I said. I didn't want Mrs Tiggy-Winkle's pink nails in my arm again.

We crept back along the passageway, tiptoeing over the brown geometric carpet. I was terrified someone would catch us. Winnie was on night duty, and once she'd finished sucking up to Jean she would be prowling around, sticking her nose in everywhere. There'd be nothing Winnie would like more than to find me and Miles out of bed, especially with a bottle of whatever-it-was shoved down the front of Miles's pyjama bottoms.

We heard footsteps.

I grabbed Miles by the arm and we pegged it into my room.

'Get under the bed!' I said as I grabbed the bottle and shoved it deep into the washing basket, while Miles struggled to fit in the narrow space under the bed.

I had just leapt onto my bed and picked up the *Who's Who* when the door opened. It was Uncle Frederick. He was redder than usual, as red as the curtains. He looked like a cooked tomato whose skin was ready to come off.

'Were you out of bed?' he said.

I tried to look as innocent as possible. I could feel Miles's knees pushing underneath the mattress.

'I've just been reading,' I said.

Uncle Frederick looked around my room suspiciously.

'I heard footsteps in the corridor,' he said.

'It might have been Winnie,' I said. 'Or one of the guests.'

Uncle Frederick sniffed the air.

'It smells of smoke in here.'

'Joseph smokes under my window – it always smells of smoke,' I replied. It's lucky I'm so good at lying, really.

Uncle Frederick looked at me steadily. Making his mind up. This is the bit I hate the most, the making-the-mind-up bit. The waiting. I thought of Miles folded up under the bed. What would he think?

Uncle Frederick took a step towards me and sat on the bed. I heard Miles gasp at the weight and coughed to cover up the sound.

Uncle Frederick took my hand. His fingers are always clammy and covered in bubbly warts.

'What are we going to do with you?' he asked.

I looked down at my nightie. You don't answer Uncle Frederick in the middle of the night, even when he asks you a question, because it's usually a trick.

'Swearing at Jean,' he said, stroking my palm. 'That wasn't very clever, was it?'

He curled my fingers into a fist, his hand around mine, and started to squeeze.

'That wasn't a very nice thing for a little girl like you to do. When your auntie and I take you in and look after you,' he said.

The joints in my knuckles were starting to sing with pain. He squeezed harder.

'Is this the sort of person we have living in our hotel?' he asked, in his low, singy-songy way. 'The sort of ungrateful little bitch who makes her auntie cry?'

I thought every bone in my hand would break. I didn't scream or say anything. I didn't want Miles to hear.

'Now, what do you say?' Uncle Frederick said.

I could barely reply through the agony.

He tried again, working my wrist now too, bending it back.

'I'm sorry!' I gasped.

There was a moment where I thought I had said the wrong thing. Sometimes Uncle Frederick wants the exact opposite of what he says.

He let go of my hand, which felt crumpled and useless with pain, like a bit of paper he'd screwed up.

'You'll be a good little girl from now on, won't you?' he asked, leaning forward and giving me one of his horrid kisses.

'Yes, Uncle,' I replied, his spit in my mouth. The burning shame was already taking over the pain in my hand. The idea that Miles could hear all this.

'Because,' he said, walking over to the door, 'you're lucky your aunt and I look after you at all. If we decided that we couldn't look after you any more . . . well, your grandmother is not in the best of health, is she? You'd be all by yourself then, and it'd be nobody's fault but your own.'

I nodded.

'Why don't you think about that, eh?' he said. 'Goodnight.'

Once the door was closed, Miles burst out from under the bed, choking for breath.

'I thought I was going to suffocate!' he said.

I'd tried to wipe the tears from my face, but Miles could see that I'd been crying.

He sat up on the bed with me. I thought for a minute he might give me a hug. I wished he would more than anything in the world.

He didn't.

'He's a bastard, isn't he?' Miles said.

I laughed. I wanted to burst into tears all over again.

'Do you want me to kill him for you?' Miles asked.

I sniffled back the tears as best as I could.

'Nah, you're all right,' I replied.

Miles slept in my bed, top to toe, and it was the only time in the last few years that I have slept for more than an hour straight.

When I woke up, he was gone, and my hand hurt.

14

Top to Toe

PC Nodder and DCI Rottman are really getting it in the neck in the papers. Even the town is starting to get sick of them. Rottman barges about the place, with Nodder arguing with him all the way, and they go round and round in circles asking everyone the same questions. Rottman is baring his teeth more than ever now, ready to snap on anything anyone says. I even saw him yelling at Cordelia Botkin's mother. Which seemed a bit much. I think the heat and the town is getting to him. In the evenings he sits by himself in the Chinese restaurant, writing furiously in his notebook. I don't think he's writing anything at all in there. He just wants us all to think he's busy while he fills himself with special fried rice.

It's pretty clear he hasn't the foggiest who the murderer is. That's the best thing about dropping a body in the sea, from a murderer's point of view – all that salt and water washes away the clues and the bodies bob up to the surface all white and clean.

Poor George Brain has gone very quiet. Mayor Hoolhouse doesn't want him ranting away on his box with reporters in the town, and Rottman is on standby to send him packing the moment he looks like he's about to do one of his speeches. He looks even more deranged than usual, as though all the words are filling up inside him and he might explode at any minute. I saw him weeping round the back of the pub while I was on my daily bin rounds (you always check the bins if there's a murder going on, just in case someone has tried to chuck away the weapon or a clue on the sly). I told him I missed his speeches, and if he liked he could do one for me. He was absolutely thrilled. We found him a cardboard box to stand on (it broke) and he kept at it for a full half-hour. He talked about the usual things, although unsurprisingly this time his number-one targets were Mayor Hoolhouse and Mr Podmore, whom he said had been murdering people together for hundreds of years. We both know that Mayor Hoolhouse is fifty, and pretty unlikely to have been around two hundred years ago, but I didn't want to ruin it while he was in the swing of things. After George Brain was finished he helped me go through the bins. We didn't find anything helpful, but we did find an old packet of out-of-date cheese-and-onion crisps, so we shared those.

I went to Peter Queen's shop to buy some marshmallows. He was quite standoffish after our tea and was pretty tight-lipped when I tried to hang around and have a chat. Eventually he gave me the marshmallows for free, just to get rid of me. I don't know what Peter Queen's problem is, I really don't. It's not like anyone else wants to talk to him, except for me, and maybe Rottman, if he's on one of his rounds.

Mrs Tiggy-Winkle has been very possessive over Miles for the past few days. She doesn't let him out of her sight for a second. He doesn't even glance at me when he's with her, while she stares at me with a gloating, frog-like smile, clutching at his shoulders like he's her prize. I don't mind it, because every night Miles comes and sleeps in my room with me. We don't even talk much, really; we just lie there, top to toe, stuck together like limpets.

I'm worried that Uncle Frederick might come in on one of his midnight visits, so I put the bin against the door to give Miles enough time to get under the bed if he does. So far we've been lucky – it's harder for Uncle Frederick to creep into my room with the hotel so full.

I've been sleeping so well that I've been skipping around town, smiling at everyone and offering to do chores to keep me busy while Miles is with his mother. Albert Fish says I'm like a different person – he even let me stick my hand in the touch pool (while he supervised)!

There is a lot of talk in the town about Regatta Week and whether it should happen because of the murders. No one seems to be able to make up their minds about this, so one day the extra bunting and Union Jack flags are strung up, and the next day they're taken down and hidden away. The Flower twins in the bookshop think it's 'distasteful' to dance about while families are grieving, but other people feel like the town deserves a bit of fun under the circumstances. I don't really mind either way, but I'm enjoying all the bickering.

Jean has been tormenting Dorothea ever since she stuck up for me in the lobby. Dorothea is doing all she can to get on Jean's good side, but even I can see that the more she tries, the more Jean enjoys batting her away. Jean has moved from the lobby to the lounge, spending her time asking Aunt Maria about Winnie, commenting on what a clever and interesting person Winnie is and saying that Aunt Maria should give her a better position.

'She could even take over your job, Maria,' Jean

says. 'I'm sure she'd find answering the phones a lot less taxing than you do.'

'I'm sure you're right, Jean,' Aunt Maria replies. 'But then, what would I do?'

'Oh,' Jean says, 'I'm sure there's something you could do.'

Poor Dorothea is agonised by these conversations, and when Aunt Maria leaves the room she says in a shaking voice that Jean should be kinder to her.

'Why must you always take her part?' Jean says. 'Honestly! You're as much of a drip as she is!'

I think Dorothea and Aunt Maria would be friends if it weren't for Uncle Frederick and Jean.

The summer is rolling on and on, sticky-hot and golden. But I'm not really interested in the daytime any more. I just wait for the sun to go down and then the night slinks in and I hear the knock on my door from Miles.

Mrs Tiggy-Winkle doesn't even suspect. Miles spends all day sucking up to her, going on endless walks and rubbing her sore feet in the parlour, and she is pink-cheeked with happiness.

I'm being extra good too, just to make extra sure not to give Uncle Frederick any reason to come to me. So far it's working, but you can never be too sure. Sometimes you never really know why Uncle Frederick comes.

15

Stupid, stupid, stupid, stupid, stupid, stupid,
stupid, stupid, stupid, stupid, stupid, stupid,
stupid, stupid, stupid, stupid, stupid, stupid,
stupid, stupid, stupid, stupid, stupid, stupid,
stupid, stupid, stupid, stupid, stupid, stupid,
stupid, stupid, stupid, stupid, stupid, stupid,
stupid, stupid, stupid, stupid, stupid, stupid,
stupid, stupid, stupid, stupid, stupid, stupid,
stupid, stupid, stupid, stupid, stupid, stupid,
stupid, stupid, stupid, stupid, stupid, stupid,
stupid, stupid, stupid, stupid, stupid, stupid,
stupid, stupid, stupid, stupid, stupid, stupid,
stupid, stupid, stupid, stupid, stupid, stupid,

stupid, stupid, stupid, stupid, stupid, stupid,
stupid, stupid, stupid, stupid, stupid, stupid,
stupid, stupid, stupid, stupid, stupid, stupid,
stupid, stupid, stupid, stupid, stupid, stupid,
stupid, stupid, stupid, stupid, stupid, stupid,
stupid, stupid, stupid, stupid, stupid, stupid,
stupid, stupid, stupid, stupid, stupid, stupid,
stupid, stupid, stupid, stupid, stupid, stupid,
stupid, stupid, stupid, stupid, stupid, stupid,
stupid, stupid, stupid, stupid, stupid, stupid,
stupid, stupid, stupid, stupid, stupid, stupid,
stupid, stupid, stupid, stupid, stupid, stupid,
stupid, stupid, stupid, stupid, stupid, stupid,
stupid, stupid, stupid, stupid, stupid, stupid,
stupid, stupid, stupid, stupid, stupid, stupid,
stupid, stupid, stupid, stupid, stupid, stupid,
stupid, stupid, stupid, stupid, stupid, stupid,
stupid, stupid, stupid, stupid, stupid, stupid,
stupid, stupid, stupid, stupid, stupid, stupid,
stupid, stupid, stupid, stupid, stupid, stupid,
stupid, stupid, stupid, stupid, stupid, stupid,
stupid, stupid, stupid, stupid, stupid, stupid,
stupid, stupid, stupid, stupid, stupid, stupid,

stupid, stupid, stupid, stupid, stupid, stupid,
stupid, stupid, stupid, stupid, stupid, stupid,
stupid, stupid, stupid, stupid, stupid, stupid,
stupid, stupid, stupid, stupid, stupid, stupid,
stupid, stupid, stupid, stupid, stupid, stupid,
stupid, stupid, stupid, stupid, stupid, stupid,
stupid, stupid, stupid, stupid, stupid, stupid,
stupid, stupid, stupid, stupid, stupid, stupid,
stupid, stupid, stupid, stupid, stupid, stupid,
stupid, stupid, stupid, stupid, stupid, stupid,
stupid, stupid, stupid, stupid, stupid, stupid,
stupid, stupid, stupid, stupid, stupid, stupid,
stupid, stupid, stupid, stupid, stupid, stupid,
stupid, stupid, stupid, stupid, stupid, stupid,
stupid, stupid, stupid, stupid, stupid, stupid,
stupid, stupid, stupid, stupid, stupid, stupid,
stupid, stupid, stupid, stupid, stupid, stupid,
stupid, stupid, stupid, stupid, stupid, stupid,
stupid, stupid, stupid, stupid, stupid, stupid,
stupid, stupid, stupid, stupid, stupid, stupid,
stupid, stupid, stupid, stupid, stupid, stupid,
stupid, stupid, stupid, stupid, stupid, stupid,
stupid, stupid, stupid, stupid, stupid, stupid.

16

A Girl in the Tide Pool

The eels are back. Cold and cold and cold and slimy and dark.

Yesterday was terrible. Miles didn't come and stay with me last night.

Yesterday morning Mrs Tiggy-Winkle had to go off to see an old school friend over in Polruan. They had arranged to have lunch together and do the Hall Walk, and according to Miles she hadn't been so excited about anything in ages. Miles knew that this was his chance to shake her off, so that morning he said he was feeling sick and that he thought he had sunstroke because of all the prickly jumpers she made him wear and begged her to let him stay in the hotel and sleep it off. And because Mrs Tiggy-Winkle loves him so much and thinks he's so fucking wonderful, she said he could.

I was so excited that we'd get to spend the day together. The plan was that once Mrs Tiggy-Winkle had got on the ferry to Polruan, Miles would leap out of bed and we'd go off to the beach.

I packed up my satchel with towels and sweeties and *The Murderers' Who's Who* and I got Joseph to make us some cheese sandwiches. I begged Aunt Maria for some extra money so that I could buy a beach ball and some rock-pool nets from the shop. I had it all planned in my head: we would poke sea anemones and go crabbing and swim out to the red buoy, and I was going to wear my new stripy swimming costume with an anchor on it that I saved up for.

Miles was as white as milk in his swimming trunks, and with his pale hair he almost glowed against the stony beach.

He was in a bad mood from the moment we set off, and it didn't matter how many sweets I offered him, or how many exciting things I had planned – he barely even bothered to respond to me. I said that I'd nick an inflatable crocodile from the beach shop and we could see how far we could float out to sea, but he just rolled his eyes, as if I'd suggested the stupidest thing in the world.

He complained about the beach, and the stones, and the seaweed, and the water being too cold. He complained about the sand not being wet enough to make proper sandcastles, and that we were too old for sandcastles anyway, and about getting sunburned, and the stickiness of the sun cream, and he teased me about how stupid my new swimming costume looked with my bruised knees and my skinny legs. He said that he was bored of the *Who's Who* and that we needed to get another murder book with better pictures in it. He was bored, bored, bored, and whatever I tried there was nothing I could do to fix it.

Eventually, almost in tears, I thought that maybe he might cheer up a bit if we went somewhere else. I suggested we go up to the tide pool. Miles agreed grudgingly, leaving me to clear up all the stuff and hobble after him over the hot pebbles.

The tide pool is about a five-minute walk from the town, and I had to run after Miles, whose legs are longer than mine and who wasn't walking slowly so that I could keep up with him. It's a shallow, concrete, rectangular pool set into the rocks just below the town. When the tide comes in, it fills up with green seawater. It's got slimy barnacles all over the bottom, but the deepest it gets is only up to your neck, so you can stand in it and keep cool. I used to swim in there when I was younger – it's safer than the sea when you're learning to swim, although a few years ago a child did get swept out to sea when a big wave crashed over him and sucked all the water out of the pool. They have railings around the outer edges now so that never happens again. Since the new sports complex opened last year, with its turquoise heated swimming pool and inflatable armbands, hardly anyone ever goes to the tide pool any more.

The pool was deserted except for one blonde girl reading a comic and paddling her feet. She was my age, maybe a bit younger, but her ears were pierced and she was wearing a pink bikini, which was string-tied at the back and the sides. She kicked her heels in the water, ignoring us. Her toenails were painted with glitter.

Miles looked at her for a moment and then jumped into the pool. She pulled her comic away so she didn't get it wet, but didn't look up from the page.

'I've got a new game,' he said to me, looking at her.

The game was a new murder game. This time, rather than being strangled, the victim was drowned. Miles would push me under the water, and I would have to thrash around, yelling and screaming, begging for my life.

But then it started getting horrid.

Miles held me under for too long. I didn't like the game. But he insisted that we do it again and again. Yanking at my hair when I refused.

The blonde girl looked at us, her head cocked.

All the thrashing around had got her attention.

'What are you doing?' she asked. She had a high voice and a thick accent from somewhere I didn't recognise.

'Playing a game,' Miles said.

'What sort of game?' she asked.

'It's something we made up together,' I told her. 'Only we can play it.'

'What are the rules?' she asked.

'It's a grown-up game,' I said. I didn't like the way Miles was looking at her.

'You can play,' he said.

'No, she can't!' I said.

'Don't be a baby,' Miles said. 'It can't just be me and you all summer, you know.'

I didn't know what to do. I stared helplessly as the girl slipped into the water and paddled towards us. She was very pretty. I knew she was prettier than me.

'I'm Mary Pearcey,' she said in her funny accent.

'Where are you from?' Miles asked.

'From Ireland,' she said. 'I'm staying up at the caravan park with my dad for our holiday.'

'You know everyone says the murderer is from the caravan park?' I said. 'It's probably your dad.'

Mary stuck out her lower lip. 'What murderer?' she said.

'See?' I said triumphantly. 'She doesn't even know about the murderer. How can she play the game?'

Miles ignored me.

'That's the game we're playing,' Miles said to her. 'We're playing Murder.'

'What game is that?' she asked.

'Well,' Miles said, drifting towards her in the water, 'I'm the murderer, and you're the victim. You have to swim around a bit, and then I grab you and you have to pretend to drown.'

Mary Pearcey thought about this for a second.

'Okay,' she said.

I couldn't believe it, Miles telling her about our game. OUR game.

Mary started swimming around, and Miles circled her like a shark. I wasn't part of the game any more. I'd been pushed to the corner.

Mary started giggling as Miles got closer and closer to her. Teasing her, getting close and then pulling away. Finally, when she was shrieking with excitement, he grabbed her leg and pulled her under.

He held her under for a moment, and then let her back up to catch her breath. She was still giggling. He pulled her down again, swishing her around, their blond hair trailing after them, their legs tangling together.

He was being gentler with her than he was with me, and she didn't struggle. They went on and on with the game. Making up new rules. Miles gave her different characters, different victims, and she had to drown in a different way depending on what he said. Sometimes she shrieked in an American accent and fought back, or she was already dead and just floating on the surface of the pool with Miles moving her, or he would let her escape the pool entirely and then he would run after her and grab her and jump in with her. They giggled away. Teasing each other. I was forgotten.

Miles even let her be the murderer for a bit – something he had never, ever let me do, no matter how hard I'd begged him.

I pressed my back against the concrete corner of the pool, rubbing up against it until I could feel the skin graze and the salt water start to sting.

Eventually, after what seemed like forever, when I was as cold and shrivelled as a fossil, the sun slipped behind some clouds and the temperature dropped. I got out of the pool and wrapped myself in my spotty beach towel. Miles didn't even notice.

A man with a deep crackling tan and a pair of fluorescent swimming shorts appeared at the top of the stairs and called down.

'Mary!' he said in the same accent as hers. 'It's late! Let's go!'

Mary dimpled at Miles like a mermaid and swam to the edge of the pool. 'Coming, Dad!' she called.

She pulled herself elegantly out of the pool, wiggling her bottom. She had a tan almost as deep as her father's, and you could see a white stripe of skin around the edge of her bikini.

She pulled her towel around her.

'Bye, Miles,' she said, batting her eyelashes at him. She didn't even look at me.

She skipped up the stairs to her father, who took her hand impatiently and they disappeared up the hill.

Miles watched them go.

'She's a very good victim,' he said. 'She makes a lot less fuss than you do.'

'I think a good victim would make a lot of fuss,' I said. 'If someone was really trying to drown you, you wouldn't just lie there like a bloody idiot, would you?'

Miles made the face he always makes when he thinks I'm behaving babyishly.

'Let's go back,' he said.

'Fine,' I said.

He smirked again.

We walked up to the hotel in total silence, shivering in the cold.

I spent all evening preparing my apology, while he sat with Mrs Tiggy-Winkle in the dining room. I didn't want him to be cross with me – I couldn't bear it – and I realised that I should have been nicer to stupid Mary. I'd be her best friend in the world if it meant that Miles would still be my friend.

I waited up and up and up. I paced around and picked my nails and read the *Who's Who* until I saw the thin green line of dawn and smelled the first cigarette of Joseph's morning.

But Miles didn't come.

17

By Myself

It's my birthday in two days. Neither Uncle Frederick nor Aunt Maria has mentioned it. There is an old antique book of ghost stories with lots of creepy illustrations and a stain on the cover that I kept hinting about, but it's still in the window of Flowers' Bookshop. I suppose I'll just have to nick it for myself.

Miles has hardly spoken to me since the day in the tide pool. Whenever I try to catch him at breakfast Mrs Tiggy-Winkle pulls him away.

There seems to be no way of talking to him. Jean is always in the parlour listening in, and even if I do manage to sneak up to him, he acts like he's desperate to get away. Like I'm some boring old drooling aunt or something.

At night I lie awake, imagining him playing the murder games with Mary from the caravan park. I wonder if he's seen her again. It's unlikely, with Mrs Tiggy-Winkle always sniffing around, but then I know that he knows how to give her the slip.

I can't even be bothered to go down to the town. I just stay in my room or kick around the hotel, hoping Miles will come and talk to me. I lie in the bath for hours, pretending I'm dead, letting my hair float around me until the water goes cold. I imagine that the murderer has got me, and I imagine what everyone will do when they hear the news, and how bad everyone will feel that they ignored me the whole time I was alive. I think of Miles, crying quietly at the back of my funeral procession through the town. But whenever I think of Miles I think of

Mary, who ducks into my thoughts and slips her hand into his.

Yesterday I stopped Arthur Rottman while he was doing his rounds. I told him that I had seen a man from the caravan park behaving strangely by the tide pool. I said he looked like he might be a pervert and that his name was Mr Pearcey. I explained that it would probably be a good idea if he questioned him, and that it might be an even better idea to shut the caravan park completely for the summer while the murder investigation was going on. Rottman seemed a bit restless and looked over my shoulder the whole time I was explaining this.

'Shouldn't you be writing all this down?' I said, pointing at his notepad. 'His name is Mr Pearcey.'

Rottman bared his teeth in that horrid smile of his and said that he wasn't writing it down because he thought I was telling lies, and that he didn't like me snooping around the town, getting in the way all the time, and that he's heard I'm not trustworthy. When I asked him where he's heard that rubbish from, he wouldn't answer.

It's all very well of Rottman to say that I'm lying and I'm a snoop, but what if I wasn't lying about Mr Pearcey? For all I know Mr Pearcey *is* a pervert and might easily be the murderer. No wonder Rottman hasn't found the culprit yet if he won't even listen when concerned civilians come up and tell him what they think!

18

The Town Meeting

It's my birthday. Thirteen. But no one has noticed because something else has happened today. I woke up thinking that maybe Aunt Maria might have remembered, or Miles, if Miles were still my friend.

But when I went downstairs wearing an extra layer of blue eyeshadow in celebration, it turned out that everyone's minds were elsewhere.

Another body has washed up, on Readymoney Beach.

Aunt Maria tried to keep it from me, but with a hotel full of journalists it's pretty tricky to keep secrets.

The body was found this morning, lying in the middle of the beach, naked and covered in seaweed. It had obviously got tangled up in some rubbish, because there was a plastic bag caught around her arm and a Coke-can ring pull in her hair. She was as bloated as the others, face down and pearl-white, according to Jean, who had heard it from someone who had been watching when they took the body away.

They haven't said who she is yet.

Rottman is furious. He can't believe a girl has been murdered right underneath his nose in a town full of police keeping watch. The evening news is full of films of Readymoney covered in police tape, and the ambulance leaving the scene, and Rottman blusteringly trying to defend himself, saying they were getting closer and closer to cracking the case.

Mayor Hoolhouse, with his wig slipping down his forehead and people pulling on his sleeves asking him what on earth they were supposed to do, decided to call an emergency meeting in the Town Hall this afternoon.

Everyone is really freaking out now. The tourists who initially found it all rather exciting have packed their bags and scarpered. Aunt Maria was weeping in the lobby in full view of the whole hotel until Uncle Frederick yanked her into his office. Winnie has now taken over reception and answers everyone's questions in the rudest possible way, rolling her eyes and snapping at people when they ask for their money back. She has propped up a little sign on the desk that read 'NO refunds' and points to it when guests get uppity with her.

The journalists are in a frenzy, rushing around, trying to swap information, desperate to get the scoop.

I don't even care about the murders any more. I don't care if every person in this town gets hauled into the sea. Without Miles to talk to about them, it's hard to get excited.

The Town Hall was stuffed with people and so hot that one old lady fainted and had to be taken outside. I pressed myself up against the wooden panelling at the back so I could get a view of the room. Everyone was there. Peter Queen, looking tearful and a bit sick; George Brain, shouting dire warnings; Albert Fish, who had shut up the aquarium so that he could attend. Jean had insisted on being taken down by Dorothea, and shooed people off with her walking stick if they got too close to her. Uncle Frederick had left Aunt Maria up at the hotel, because she was likely to burst into tears again and cause a scene. Mrs Tiggy-Winkle and Miles weren't there. I thought Miles would have come – I knew he would have liked to see everyone all in a tizz like this, but his mother must have dragged him off on one of their day trips. I noticed Mr Pearcey in the crowd too, wearing a pink shirt with a great sweat patch on his back. Mary wasn't with him. I wondered if Mary and Miles were together, and nearly picked the whole nail off my thumb thinking about it.

DCI Rottman stood on the small wooden stage underneath the huge portrait of Her Majesty the Queen, shouting to be heard. A couple of new policemen were standing behind him, looking itchy in their wool uniforms, and PC Nodder had a sort of 'I-told-you-so' look on his face. The big-shot policeman from London didn't know any more than he did, and he looked thrilled about it, not minding, really, that someone else had to get murdered to prove his point.

'Why haven't you found him yet?' someone yelled from the crowd.

'We are following up on a few leads,' Rottman shouted over the din. 'It's only a matter of time until we catch the culprit.'

'What's taking so long?' someone else called.

Rottman bristled. 'Murder investigations are not simple. It's a complicated process. But mark my words, we're getting closer every day.'

'Do you know who it is then?' Mr Pearcey shouted. 'Some of us have got kids here. It's not safe.'

'The town is perfectly safe,' said Rottman. There was a roar from the crowd. People started laughing and jeering at him. 'The town is perfectly safe,' he said more loudly, with a toothy grimace, 'as long as you are all vigilant. I would ask you all to report anyone you think is behaving suspiciously.'

'It's a bit late for that!' a woman shouted.

PC Nodder watched with pleasure as Rottman tried to pacify the furious mob of people. Mayor Hoolhouse stepped forward, straightening his cravat.

'Now, now,' he said, putting up a manicured hand. 'This is no way to behave, is it? Making a scene in the Town Hall! What would Mr Podmore think?'

The hall quietened down immediately.

'I don't think Mr Podmore would be very proud of our little town if he saw us all shouting at poor Mr Rottman.'

'*DCI* Rottman,' Rottman hissed.

Mayor Hoolhouse gave him a cool smile.

'Indeed,' Mayor Hoolhouse said. 'Now, I am sure the police are doing all they can.'

The crowd looked like it might start up again.

'Uh, uh, uh,' Mayor Hoolhouse said, waggling his finger. 'We must all keep calm. We must all bear in mind that the eyes of the country are trained on our streets.'

He looked pointedly at a group of journalists frantically scribbling in their books.

'Now, we can all admit that what has happened this summer has been . . . unfortunate. But there is no need for us all to turn on one another. We must pull together! Lest we forget, Regatta Week is only a few weeks away.'

'Regatta Week?' someone shouted. 'We can't do Regatta Week!'

Mayor Hoolhouse glared at the culprit.

'Of course we can! Regatta Week has been our tradition for years. What this town needs is something to focus on, to remind us all what we're about!'

'It's disgusting!' a voice rang out from the back. It was George Brain.

Mayor Hoolhouse smiled. 'Let's not have one of your dreary rants, George,' he said. 'Not today.'

'I told you!' George yelled. 'I knew there would be mermaids washed up on the rocks. Didn't I tell you?'

'Yes, you did,' Mayor Hoolhouse answered. 'And I wonder, George, how did you know?'

The room was silent. Heads turned to look at George.

'What?' George said. 'What do you mean?'

'I mean,' Mayor Hoolhouse replied, with a half-smile, 'that it's an awful coincidence that you predicted all of this.'

Rottman whispered something in one of his policemen's ears.

'I see what you're doing,' George said nervously. 'Don't listen to him! He's rotten! He's as rotten as all of you.'

DCI Rottman stepped off the stage, with his men walking behind him.

'It's not me! It's not me!' George cried.

George Brain looked desperately at the crowd, who were starting to shy away from him, and then at the door. Then he bolted.

People started screaming. A few men tried to grab at his stained jacket as he passed, but he wrenched free and ran through the door. Rottman and his men broke into a run, chasing after him. I stuck my foot out and caught one of the policemen on his shiny black boot. He went flying onto the floor.

The whole crowd ran out into the street to watch Rottman as he chased after George Brain. George Brain's shoes had holes in them and were slippery, and, as always, he was drunk and not really running in a straight line.

Rottman caught up with him and roughly pulled his arm behind his back.

'No!' George cried. 'It's not me!'

It was too late. The crowd was against him; the journalists were taking photographs, unable to believe their luck.

George struggled against Rottman and started trying to spit on him, until the policeman I'd tripped up arrived and bashed him over the head with his truncheon.

The crowd cheered.

'Well,' I heard Mayor Hoolhouse say to his wife, 'that's that then.'

Everyone stayed on the street long after the police car had driven off with George Brain crying in the back seat. It was almost like a party. The landlord of the Anchor came out with trays of drinks. No one seemed to mind that they'd just grabbed George for the sake of it, because he talks too much and smells a bit. Jean said loudly that she'd known all along, that she'd always thought there was something funny about him and that she hoped he would rot in hell for what he'd done to those poor girls – and that the press could quote her on that.

Mayor Hoolhouse told everyone that he'd suspected it for quite some time himself, but that they all had to let the police do their job. He said he would write the news personally to Mr Podmore, and that he was sure Mr Podmore would be very pleased.

A woman wearing dungarees and thick glasses said that she'd seen George Brain down at the beach early this morning. She'd been walking her dog – a toothless pug that she pushed around in a child's pram – and hadn't thought anything of it until she heard about the body. Personally I wouldn't trust anyone who carted their dog around like a baby, but everyone started to crowd around her and asked her to tell them what George had been doing.

'I thought he was looking for shells,' she said, pushing her glasses up her nose. 'He was rooting around in the seaweed.'

'Did you see the body?' Mayor Hoolhouse asked.

'Well . . . no . . .' she said. The crowd seemed disappointed. 'But it might have been behind some sand, mightn't it? I couldn't be sure from the angle. But he certainly seemed shifty. Didn't we think so, Professor Cuddles?'

She tickled her pug under his chin.

'Yes, we did,' she said in a baby voice. 'We thought he looked very shifty.'

Professor Cuddles didn't really look like he had an opinion either way, and buried his head in his basket.

'I think you ought to go and tell DCI Rottman what you saw,' Mayor Hoolhouse said, leaning towards her conspiratorially. 'You may hold the key to this entire investigation.'

The woman blushed.

'Me?' she said. 'Speak to DCI Rottman! Well, yes, yes, I should!'

She thrust Professor Cuddles's basket at the Mayor so that she could comb her hair with her fingers.

'I suppose I do hold the key, Mayor Hoolhouse,' she said proudly. 'I suppose I do.'

Poor George Brain.

19

Birthday Present

When I got back to my room after tea there was a present sitting on my bed. A square box, wrapped in yellow spotty paper.

Maybe Aunt Maria had remembered after all! Or maybe Joseph had made me a cake! My hands were shaking as I walked up to it.

There was no card, just a bit of ribbon holding the paper together. I could hardly untie the bow – my fingers got all in a muddle.

A fur hat! I thought when I looked inside. It

seemed like a bit of an odd present, considering it was the middle of burning summer, but I wasn't going to complain. A present is a present!

But when I touched it, I realised it wasn't a hat.

I pulled my arm out of the box. I recognised the fur. Patchy and yellow. Then I noticed the smell.

It was Fucko the cat.

He was folded up in the bottom of the box. He wasn't floppy like a sleeping cat, but stiff, like he'd been stuffed with cardboard, and his face looked all slack.

I saw that there was a string around his neck, with a note attached to it.

Happy Birthday, it said. There was a paw print drawn next to it.

Miles. It had to be. I didn't know what to think about it. It seemed like just the sort of joke that Miles would make, and it was quite funny, really, when I thought about it. But I put the lid back on the box all the same; I didn't like to look at Fucko with his tail all crooked and his teeth bared.

There was a knock on the door and there he was, suddenly in my doorway, as though he'd never ignored me at all and we'd been friends all along.

He seemed almost shy, looking down at his feet.

'Thank you for my present,' I said. I didn't know what else to say, really. 'Why did you give me a dead cat for my birthday?' seemed a bit rude.

'You're welcome,' he said. 'I thought you'd like it. You were always banging on about how much you hated that stupid cat so . . .'

'Yeah, I was . . .' I agreed. It was actually Miles who really hated the cat and chased him around the lobby trying to stomp on his tail, but I didn't want to ruin the moment.

'You didn't –' I laughed nervously. 'You didn't do it, did you?'

Miles didn't say anything. His eyes are so grey sometimes that they look almost white. He shifted his feet, in the impatient way he does when I'm being slow or babyish. I got the feeling suddenly that the present was a test, and I'd got it wrong somehow.

'Because it would be funny if you did!' I blurted out. I didn't want Miles to go away. To stop talking to me. I wanted him to come back and start sleeping in my bed again.

'No,' Miles said finally. 'I found him in the garden this morning.'

'Cool,' I said, like I didn't even care either way.

'I knew you'd think it was funny.' He seemed pleased. 'I knew you would.'

He came and sat on my bed next to the box.

'There's something else in there too,' he said.

I looked at the box. I didn't really want to put my hand in there again. Miles seemed to sense my hesitation.

'Oh, don't be pathetic,' he said. 'It's only a bit of old fluff.'

I opened the box. I didn't want Miles to be disappointed, so I did it as coolly as I could. There was a moment when I thought it might be a trap. Like there might be something in there that might cut me or bite me.

Miles was smiling. I pushed the feeling down, down, down and plunged my hand in.

I hated the feeling of the fur, and the cold skin underneath it. I reached underneath and my fingers caught on the claws, and I felt the rough, sandpapery pads of the paw. I wanted to yank out my hand, but I knew that if I did that would be it, and Miles would know I was a baby once and for all. I squeezed my eyes shut and felt around the bottom of the box. Finally I found what he was talking about and pulled it out as quick as I could.

It was the book of ghost stories.

I didn't know what to do.

'I heard you talking to your aunt about it in the lobby,' Miles said. 'But I didn't think she'd remember so . . .'

This was better even than Mr West's T-shirt. This was better than anything that had ever happened.

'Open it,' he said.

Inside, on the front page, he had written: *To my best friend, love from Miles.*

Best Friend.

My Best Friend Miles.

I felt completely silly. Like I might burst into tears or jump onto him or start laughing hysterically.

Instead, I said, 'Let's throw the cat off the cliff, give him a burial at sea.'

Jean spotted us walking through the lobby on our way out to the garden.

'What are you two doing?' she asked. 'What's in the box?'

'It's my birthday present,' I said proudly.

'Birthday?' Jean said. 'It's not your birthday!'

'Yes, it is!' I said.

'Happy birthday!' Dorothea said.

'Oh, do stop, Dorothea!' Jean said. 'It isn't her birthday, is it, Maria?'

Aunt Maria stood pale behind the desk.

'I . . . I don't know . . .' she said.

Even Jean seemed to be lost for words at this.

'With the body on the beach . . . I . . .' Aunt Maria stopped. She started flicking though the desk diary frantically. 'What date is it?'

Dorothea looked at me, shocked.

'Oh, you poor thing,' she said quietly.

'I don't care,' I said, tossing my head snootily so they could see how much I didn't care.

'Miles got me a present.'

'What did Miles get you?' Dorothea said in her kindest voice.

'A dead cat,' I replied.

It took them all a moment to realise what I'd said.

Dorothea looked stung.

Jean started sputtering with rage.

'You're a foul, FOUL little girl!' Jean said. 'And a dirty little liar too. I bet that box is empty. I bet it isn't even your real birthday!'

Miles and I ran off to the garden. Aunt Maria was too embarrassed to run after us.

We clambered down a bit of the cliff so that no one could see what we were doing, and I turned the box over. Fucko bounced down the rocks and landed in the sea with a sploosh! We sat on the edge for a bit, watching the sun go down.

'You know they found out who the girl was?' Miles said.

'Who?' I asked.

'I overheard it in the parlour. The journalist with the teeth was talking about it.'

'And . . .?'

'It was Belle Gunness.'

I whistled. Belle Gunness was at the top of our victim list. She was the pretty girl who worked in the bank and smoked clove cigarettes. We were obviously pretty good at this murderer lark. Rottman should get us on his team.

'They arrested George Brain,' I said.

'The loony on the box?'

'Someone saw him on the beach this morning.'

'Do you think he did it?'

'I don't think so. I like George.'

Miles nodded.

'What's that?' he said, pointing along the cliff at a square concrete building with two slits for windows.

'It's one of the pillboxes,' I said. 'They used them during the war. Had snipers in them guarding the estuary.'

'Have you ever been in it?' he asked.

'Nope. You can only get to it by boat. Then you have to climb up. It's quite steep.'

'I'd like to be a sniper,' Miles said, turning his

finger into a gun and pointing it at a boat below. 'No one would even know you were there, then BANG!'

There was a rustling from the garden above us. We turned to see Winnie peering down crossly.

'What are you two little monsters doing now?' she asked. 'Miles, your mother's going mad looking for you in the hotel. Get up here.'

Miles got up, brushing the grass off his bottom.

'See you,' he said. 'Happy birthday.'

'Happy birthday,' Winnie mimicked with a sneer.

But even Winnie and her stupid face couldn't make me feel cross.

Not with my Best Friend Miles near me.

20

The Murder Tour

They haven't let George Brain go yet. He's still in the police station, answering questions. Rottman is certain that he is the murderer. Everyone is certain he's the murderer. The whole town feels transformed. Everyone is so full of excitement and relief that they're practically spinning about and singing. Some are a bit disappointed that this means all the excitement has finished – after all, without the murders going on, what will everyone talk about? No one seems to have considered the idea that it might not be George Brain at all. As far as Fowey is concerned, George is guilty and that's that.

Mr Podmore is very pleased.

He sent a letter to everyone in the town, on stiff white card edged in gold, congratulating them all on how very, very well they have done under the circumstances. Mr Podmore was very proud, but also wanted to remind everyone that even though they had pleased him very greatly, and been a tribute to him and the Podmore name, they must also be reminded that the press was still at large in the town, and they must not let standards slip.

The Flower twins have framed the letter and put it above their desk in the shop.

Everyone is getting things spruced up for Regatta Week, making glittery banners and painting over the rust on the bollards and railings on the quay. The town band keeps playing 'I Vow to Thee, My Country' over and over again to get it perfect for the big parade. I wish someone would shove something down the tuba to get them to stop.

People already talk about the murders as if they are something that happened years ago. But Belle Gunness is still in the morgue, and her family move around the town like ghosts, trying to grasp hold of what has happened to them.

They say something was in her mouth. Another stone.

Mrs Tiggy-Winkle has caught the flu. She started being sick yesterday morning and has been in her bedroom with the curtains drawn for two full days. She'd have made Miles sit next to her and hold her hand if she wasn't so terrified of giving it to him. She made Miles promise that he wouldn't go 'gallivanting about with that awful girl' (me), so he promised her and hoped to die.

We have spent the last two days together.

Since George Brain 'The Murderer' has been imprisoned, a whole river of fascinated people has flooded the town. People were a bit nervous about coming while they might still get murdered, but now it's an absolute free-for-all. They poke around Readymoney Beach, peer into the water of the quay and shudder, and then go off and get an ice cream.

Miles suggested we start doing a tour, since we know more than anyone else about the Fowey murders – and murders in general, from everything we've learned from the *Who's Who*. I could do all the talking, Miles said, because I like talking, and he could collect the money and make sure everything ran smoothly. We borrowed some paint from Albert Fish, who was painting the aquarium door so that it looked nice and shiny for the regatta. We got a bit of old wood from the bins round the back of the pub and painted a sign.

It said: MURDER TOURS, £2.

Miles said it needed something to make it seem more official, so we added: LEARN FROM THE EXPERTS.

I painted a few spiders and skulls on it, just to give it a bit more pizzazz, and we propped it up on the wall by the quay and waited.

It hardly took any time at all until we had someone come up. He was a man on his own, not old, but very bald. He asked us what kind of tour it was, so I explained that we'd take him to all the murder sites, and chuck in a few more general murders too to keep things moving along. He said we looked like kids, and I said that we knew more than anyone in the town about the murders, because we'd been there all along and seen it all happen. After a bit of considering, the man decided to join us and waited by the side while we tried to get more customers. Once you've got one person interested, suddenly they all turn up, and soon we had nine people wanting to come along.

They all looked like they'd got the bus in for the day and had cameras around their necks. I don't know why they bothered with the cameras; it wasn't likely that someone was going to get murdered in front of them so they could get a good snap. Miles went around the group collecting their money. One man tried to get a discount for himself and his wife, but Miles managed to stare him down and he grudgingly handed over four pounds in pennies and silver coins.

It all got off to a pretty swinging start. We took them through the town, and I told them to imagine that this was where the murderer dragged the bodies over the cobblestones. There was a bit of red paint on the wall of the Post Office, which I told them was a blood splatter, so they all took turns in taking pictures of it. We climbed down the slimy steps of the quay and I talked about the first victim, and how she was all swollen up and blue and that parts of her kept falling off. Some of the group got a bit upset and the man with the coins asked me not to be quite so gruesome, but I told him that if he wanted a less exciting tour then it wasn't my fault and he could just go off and do it by himself. His wife told him to shut up.

I explained to them about George Brain, and I gave him a hunchback and a glass eye to make him sound scarier. I pointed out the place where he had got arrested, and said he had shouted that he wouldn't rest until the whole town was murdered and at the bottom of the sea. I pointed up to the wall of old Podmore's house and told them it was an insane asylum, and that there were no doors or windows because the people inside it were so dangerous they could never be let out.

'But I can see a door there!' the bald man said. I ignored him. Some people just do not have any imagination.

I showed them the disused toilet and said it was where the murderer went to defile the bodies. I like the word 'defile', and tried to pepper it into the tour as much as I could.

'What kind of defiling did he do in the toilets?' a woman asked, her voice squeaking with excitement.

'Oh, you know,' I said enigmatically. 'The usual thing.'

Everyone nodded.

Lots of people in the group got very razzed up and wanted to have their picture taken in the toilet, so Miles and I waited around outside while they did that. The husband and wife took a lot of photos of themselves kissing in front of the loo stall, which didn't seem like a very romantic setting, especially when you take into account all the defiling that I said went on in there.

We took them up to the Town Hall and let them have a poke around there. I told them that in the olden days it had been used for satanic rituals, and that they had once found the skeletons of children under the floorboards. One of the women on the tour nodded and said she felt a strange presence in the room, and that all the dead children would probably explain it. Miles had to hide his giggles in his sleeve.

We walked over to Readymoney Beach, while I explained about all the different hauntings and savage attacks and maimings and arson that had plagued the town for centuries. I pointed out an old telephone box and told them that it rang in the middle of the night, and if you ever answered it something terrible would happen to you. They liked that a lot and took a load of photos pretending to be on the phone. I prayed it would ring, just to give them a fright.

At Readymoney I showed them where the body had been found and said that the murderer had carved a bloody message on it. A lady pointed to a bit of rust-coloured sand and asked if that was her blood. Miles and I agreed that it probably was.

We took them back to the quay where we had first started the tour, and I was just about to tell them about the cursed, phantom-infested lighthouse that had been knocked down when Mayor Hoolhouse stormed over, shouting at us to stop.

He had seen our sign and was very cross about it indeed. He started yelling at me, as though it were only my fault. Miles blended into the crowd and pretended to be looking at one of the posters for the regatta.

'You can't go around doing murder tours of the town!' Hoolhouse said, his face getting very hot. 'It's indecent!'

'What's indecent is you keeping all those poor people in the asylum with no doors!' one of the ladies in the group piped up.

'What?' Hoolhouse said. 'What asylum?'

I pretended to burst into tears to distract him. I said I was sorry that I had been showing people around the town, but that I didn't think I was doing any harm and I only did it because I needed a bit of pocket money.

Hoolhouse looked a bit embarrassed – it didn't look good for a mayor to go around shouting at young girls.

'Now then,' he said, patting me a bit awkwardly on my head. 'There's no harm done, I suppose.'

I sniffled tragically.

'None of you is a journalist, I hope?' he said to the group nervously. They shook their heads.

'Good, good,' he said, relieved. 'Now why don't you give these nice people back their money?' he said to me.

'What?' I said. 'No! That tour was an hour long!'

'Then that might teach you not to make money from other people's misery,' Hoolhouse said. 'What would Mr Podmore say? I dread to think!'

'I don't care what Mr Podmore would say!'

'Oh my goodness! Oh my goodness!' he said, looking behind him as though Podmore was standing there. 'You just be quiet now!'

He was aware that things had slipped a little out of his control.

'Right!' he said in his loudest mayor voice. 'Tour's over. Off you go!'

'But what about our money?' the bald man said.

'No time for that,' Hoolhouse snapped. 'You've had your tour. You just be on your way now.'

The group grumblingly disbanded and walked off. Miles disappeared around the corner with them.

The Mayor looked down at me. 'I don't want to catch you doing this ever again, do you understand?'

I nodded.

'Where are you from anyway?' he asked.

'I'm staying up at The Cliff Hotel,' I said.

Hoolhouse studied my face.

'You're Frederick Manning's niece!' he said.

'No!' I answered, a little too fast.

'Yes, you are! I've seen you before! Sneaking about the town. Your uncle will be hearing about this, mark my words. I'm calling him this very instant.'

I grabbed his mint-green sleeve. 'Please don't tell him,' I said. 'Please don't.'

The Mayor shook me off and walked away.

Miles appeared from out of the ice-cream shop carrying two ice creams. I turned on him and knocked one of the cones out of his hand.

'Oi!' Miles said.

'Thanks a lot!' I shouted. 'Why did you just stick me in it?'

'Didn't see the point in both of us getting caught.' Miles shrugged.

'Mayor Hoolhouse is going to tell Uncle Frederick!' I said.

'So?'

'You won't be able to stay in my room tonight,' I said.

'Why not?' he asked. He didn't realise what he'd done. I couldn't tell him.

'Just . . . because.'

'Because why?'

'Because!'

Miles watched me, thinking. Then he worked it out. We just stood there for a bit. I don't think he knew what to do.

'Can't you just lock your door?' he said finally.

'No,' I said. 'He has the door cards to all the rooms.'

There was a fishing boat coming into the harbour. The sun was starting to go down.

Miles handed his ice cream to me.

21

The Snail

Mrs Tiggy-Winkle is still vomiting into a bucket
bought specially for her in the tackle shop. She
can no longer make it to the bathroom, so she
just lies on her bed, moaning. Winnie won't go
in there any more because she says the smell is
frightful and she doesn't get paid the minimum
wage to scrub chunks out of the carpet.

Mary Pearcey has been hanging around the
hotel. She keeps asking her father to bring her
for tea, then she sits in the parlour, gazing at

Miles, licking cream off her fingers like a cat. I've been saying that I think Mary is boring and has cross-eyes, and is generally a weedy wet. Miles doesn't really say anything, he just watches her. I am trying to remind myself that I am Miles's best friend, I am the one he gave a special book of ghost stories to, and he only played with Mary once at the tide pool. It doesn't stop me feeling ill when I see them looking at each other, though.

Mary walks around like a grown-up, swinging her hips like Winnie does. She wears pink ruffled dresses and flip-flops that you can hear scraping and slapping along the lobby floor. I feel a bit stupid in my Vlad T-shirt and my old corduroy skirt, even when I do have the lovely eyeshadow on. The next time I pass the pharmacy I am going to get some glittery hairclips and lipstick, and maybe something for my fingernails too. They're short because of all the biting, and quite bleedy, but a bit of purple nail polish will make all the difference. I am thirteen now – I need to start looking a bit more high-end.

Miles and I had planned to go and have a poke around the old quarry. We'd heard it was only an hour's walk from the hotel. The police have already looked it over as a potential murder site, but we thought it might be worth having a check ourselves, just in case they missed something, which, seeing as it's Rottman and Nodder, seemed pretty likely.

I'd packed us some sweets and water for the journey, which I'd left in my room, but when I got down to the lobby, Miles was talking to Mary. She had to stand on her tiptoes to talk to him, and was giggling like an idiot already.

Her father hovered nearby, checking his watch.

'Please can I go with them, Dad?' Mary asked her father as I approached.

'I don't know, Mary, love,' Mr Pearcey said. 'We were going to have tea here, weren't we?'

'I'm bored of tea, Dad,' Mary said, putting her lip out. 'I want to go on a walk with these two.'

Mr Pearcey looked at Miles and me.

'How old are you?' he asked.

'Forty,' I said.

Miles elbowed me.

'We're twelve,' Miles said, which seemed a bit silly since we are both thirteen now, but maybe he had forgotten.

'And where are you walking to?' Mr Pearcey asked.

'We're going to catch wild boar in the woods,' I said.

'No, we aren't,' Miles said. 'We're going up to look at the quarry.'

'That doesn't sound safe, Mary,' Mr Pearcey said.

'Don't worry!' Miles said in a very responsible voice. 'We go up there all the time, it's very safe.'

'It's quite far to walk, though,' I said. 'And the murderer might still be at large.'

'Don't be silly,' Miles said. 'They've caught the murderer. And the walk isn't far at all.'

I shot a look at Miles. I didn't want stupid Mary coming with us, slowing us down.

'Please, Dad!' Mary begged in a baby voice. *'Please!'*

Mr Pearcey looked agonised. He obviously didn't like saying no to Mary, but he didn't want her to fall down the quarry either.

'Well, all right,' he said. 'As long as you're back by seven. I'll come back here to meet you.'

'Oh, thank you, Daddy!' Mary said, throwing her arms around her father and covering his face with kisses.

I stormed off ahead. If Miles wanted to spend the afternoon with Mary so much then he could bloody well wait for her to trip along in her flip-flops. I could hear them whispering the whole way to the quarry, through the cow fields and along the path where the wild horses stand in your way and look like they might bite you as you walk past.

'I don't like them, Miles,' I heard Mary whine as a scabby piebald sniffed at her skirt. Miles shooed the old horse away, and Mary hung onto his arm for the rest of the trip, pretending to be scared. I kept on calling back at them to hurry up. Mary kept on giggling and whispering things in Miles's ear, which he had to bend down to hear. He laughed too, and I started to think they were talking about me. Mary would be lucky if I didn't hurl her down the quarry myself when we got there.

The quarry wasn't really much to look at. Just a huge, gaping pit of grey stone, with a few old bits of equipment rusting away at the sides. I thought there might have been water at the bottom of it, but it must have evaporated in the heat, because the whole place was as dry as ash. A digger had been left in the middle, with all the stuffing springing out of its leather seat and its toothy bucket still half in the ground.

Mary had some trouble getting down into the pit in her flip-flops and kept slipping on the gravel, clutching at Miles to keep her steady.

Mary looked around and wrinkled her nose.

'Why did you want to come here?' she said.

'Because we're collecting clues about the murders,' I replied.

'They've already got the murderer, silly,' she said.

Miles walked over to the digger and looked inside the cabin. 'Do you think it still works?' he asked. 'There are some keys in the ignition.'

'Give it a try!' I said.

Miles climbed in. He turned the keys a couple of times. The engine made a choking, spluttering sound. He tried again, turning the key for longer. It choked again and then rumbled into life.

'Turn it off!' Mary said. 'It's dangerous!'

'Shut up, Mary,' I said. 'Do it, Miles!'

Miles started pulling at the levers and pressing his foot down on the pedals. The robotic arm moved, rising from the ground a couple of inches.

'Be careful!' Mary said. Miles couldn't hear her over the engine.

He fiddled about with the levers and the arm swung up, spraying gravel everywhere. The bucket stopped in the air in front of him.

'Hey, Mary!' Miles shouted. 'I reckon you're small enough to fit inside the bucket.'

Mary looked at the rusty thing, with its jagged edge.

'I don't think I could!' Mary said.

'Yeah, you could!' Miles said. 'If I just get it closer to the ground, you climb on and sit in it.'

'No,' Mary said. 'I don't want to.'

'Come on!' I teased. 'It'll be just like the dipper at the fair. Miles can give you a spin.'

Mary started to look a bit panicked.

'I'll get my dress all dirty,' she said.

'Never mind that!' Miles said. He manoeuvred the arm jerkily so that it was closer to the ground. Mary turned to me.

'He isn't going to make me, is he?' she said. She was frightened now.

'I don't know,' I shrugged. What did I care if Mary got her dress dirty?

Miles got out of the cabin, the engine still on. Mary backed away.

'No,' she said, tripping on her shoes. 'I really don't want to.'

Miles ran after her and scooped her up. She started scratching at his back. She was in tears now.

'Stop it!' she screamed. 'Stop, Miles!'

Miles carried her towards the bucket.

'Do you want to go in?' he asked.

'No!' she shouted. 'Please don't!'

Miles held onto her as she struggled, shrieking, in his arms. I wondered if he was really going to do it. It probably was quite dangerous, and Miles didn't really know how to work the digger at all. Mary might fall out and get crushed. I didn't say anything, though.

Miles tried to put Mary down, but she clung to him like a cat, yelping.

'All right!' Miles snapped. 'All right! If you're going to be such a baby about it.'

He let her go and she dropped onto the gravel, shaking and snivelling. Miles looked down at her, bored.

I dithered for a moment. Mary is terrible, but I didn't want her going off and telling her dad on us. Miles and I would be done for if she did – even though it would be two against one, I knew everyone would believe Mary, with her long eyelashes and her dimples. I decided to be a grown-up about it and knelt down beside her.

'Miles was only kidding, Mary,' I said. 'He wasn't really going to do it.'

Miles walked over to the digger to turn off the engine, annoyed, his game ruined.

'We were only playing a joke on you,' I said.

Mary looked at me. She didn't look half so pretty after crying. Snot was all over her face and her nose was blotchy and red.

'Do you want some sweets?' I asked. I brought out some sherbet lemons from my satchel.

Mary sniffed and took some.

'Don't people play jokes like that at your school?' I said.

'No,' Mary said quietly.

'You didn't really think Miles was going to hurt you, did you?'

Mary looked over at Miles. He smiled at her, nice and wide.

Mary wiped her eyes. She looked a bit embarrassed now that she knew she wasn't going to be put in the digger after all.

'No,' she said. 'I didn't! I knew you were joking!'

Miles came and sat on the ground with us.

'Friends again?' Miles asked, all warm and friendly. He stuck his hand out towards Mary.

'Friends,' she agreed, and shook his hand.

We snuck around the quarry for a bit, playing Kick the Can with an old bucket and seeing who could race up the side of the quarry the fastest. Even giving me and Mary a head start, Miles came first by miles. We poked around for any murder clues, but couldn't see anything obvious.

Miles found a snail dribbling over a broken spade. We tried to get it to eat a leaf, but the snail got scared and curled back into its shell.

Miles put the snail on the palm of his hand to examine it. I told him that snails didn't like hands, because of the salt from the sweat and because our skin is too hot for them. Miles didn't listen.

'You know,' he said, poking the snail with his finger, 'if you ever have ants in the kitchen in the summer, if you turn on the hob, turn it up really high and put the ants on it, their legs burn off before they can run away.'

Mary grimaced. 'That's horrible,' she said.

'No, it's not,' Miles replied. 'It's funny.'

I laughed. It did sound funny, I suppose. All the little ants trying to run away, dancing on the surface as their legs burned off.

'Then their bodies land on the hob and they go pop, pop, pop. Like popcorn,' Miles said.

The snail was trying to glide down his wrist. He picked it up and put it back in the middle of his palm.

'Snails are clever,' Miles said. 'They have an exoskeleton.'

'What does exoskeleton mean?' Mary asked.

'It means their bones are on the outside, to protect them. Their shell works like armour against predators. They can curl up inside it if something tries to hurt them, or if the sun gets too hot and they need shade.'

He poked at one of the snail's antennae, and it shot back inside its shell.

'Oh, don't do that!' Mary said. 'That's its eye! You'll hurt it!'

Miles ignored her.

'Humans have got it all the wrong way round: soft on the outside, hard on the inside – it doesn't make sense,' he said, his finger tracing the curl on the snail's back.

'We'd all look a bit stupid carting around shells on our backs,' I said.

'But then if something comes along and breaks

a snail's shell, do you know what happens?' Miles said.

Mary and I shook our heads.

'They dry out in the sun. All the goo that you see trailing behind them, it evaporates and they shrivel up like walnuts.'

Miles started to squeeze the shell with his fingers.

Mary put out her hand to stop him, and he brushed her away. The shell was harder than it looked. Miles made a fist and squeezed harder. I thought of Uncle Frederick.

'Don't, Miles,' I said, before I could stop myself.

Miles smirked at me and opened his palm – the snail's shell was still intact. Though the snail had curled up into itself in terror.

'God, you two,' Miles said. 'You're such babies.'

He dropped the snail onto the ground and, with one stomp of his shoe, shattered it. The snail writhed around, the shards of its shell sticking into its soft, grey body. Bubbles of mucus frothed out of its frilled underside.

'Why did you do that?' Mary said, her breathing uneven.

'It's just a snail, Mary,' Miles said. 'Don't be pathetic.'

'I don't care,' I said. 'Snails are stupid anyway.'

Miles smiled approvingly.

'Exactly.'

Miles and I walked up ahead on the path back to the hotel, with Mary hurrying along behind us. Mary didn't like being left out, so she pretended she didn't mind about the snail really. She likes Miles – I could tell from her moony eyes – and didn't want him to think she was a wettie. It's too late for that, I thought, and put my arm in his like she had on the way over.

Back at the hotel, Mr Pearcey was waiting in the lobby. Mary ran up to him and gave him a huge hug.

'Hello, love,' he said. 'Did you all have a nice afternoon?'

Miles and I watched Mary for her response.

'Yes, Daddy,' she said.

'Maybe you can all go off again,' he said. 'It's nice for you to have friends here, isn't it?'

Mary looked at Miles with her great big eyes. She seemed unsure.

'Yes, Daddy,' she said.

22

The Peller

Mrs Tiggy-Winkle has started to feel much better. She's making her way down to the dining room for lunch occasionally to slurp up a bit of soup before going back up to her room. Miles and I are going to have to be cleverer about how we give her the slip from now on. I am in Miles's good books since Mary was so disappointing in the quarry, and now he wants to spend all his time with me.

I thought I knew quite a lot about nature, but I'm not a patch on Miles, who knows the Latin names for plants and trees and recites them for me as we go on our walks.

We did the Hall Walk today, where you go all the way through the woods around the river and end up in Polruan, the town opposite Fowey. The Hall Walk is usually packed with people walking along in multicoloured outdoor jackets with the National Trust map in their hands, but it was raining today, so it was just me and Miles and a few dog walkers. The smell of wild garlic (or *Allium ursinum*) is even more powerful in the rain, so sickly-sweet it gets to the back of your throat. Miles told me that people die every year mistaking poisonous lily-of-the-valley leaves for wild garlic. I ate one of the leaves to show him I'm not scared.

We wondered if the Hall Walk was where Mr Queen's wife was walking her dog when she tipped over and drowned. It didn't look like there was anywhere you could easily slip and fall in the water, but then Miles and I think Mrs Queen was also murdered, so that would make sense.

We played a few rounds of the murder game. I am getting better and better at being the victim and can even cry real tears now. But then Miles is getting better at being the murderer too and sometimes hurts me, so I don't have to try too hard to cry.

When we came out of the woods we crossed the little bridge over the thin, pebbled brook. On the other side of the bridge is a small thatched cottage. Ribbons strung with bundles of dried sage and stones hang in the doorway. It sits in a sea of nodding cowslips, which smell like hot-water-bottle rubber. And today there was something new: some of its windows had been broken in.

'What's this?' Miles asked.

'It's the Peller's house,' I whispered. 'It's where the Peller lives.'

'What's a Peller?'

'A healer. Sort of. But more like a witch.'

'It looks empty,' Miles said. 'Let's go inside.'

I've never liked the Peller's house. I usually run past it when I do the walk on my own, and try not to look in its windows. I didn't want to say this because I knew it would only annoy Miles.

'There's nothing in there,' I said. 'Let's go and play the game again. There are some old ruins further up. We can play it there.'

'I'm bored of the game,' Miles said. 'I want to go in.'

We heard movement inside the house. I grabbed Miles's hand.

'Come on,' I said. I didn't want to sound panicky, but I didn't fancy getting a curse either. Miles stayed put.

'Hello?' he called.

There was a little tinkling sound and the door opened with a scrape. Even Miles jumped a bit.

An old woman peered out. She had long, orangey-grey hair and was wearing a tie-dyed skirt and a thousand necklaces. One of them seemed to be made of snail shells, strung along a length of ribbon. She looked like every picture of a witch I'd ever seen – she didn't have a wart, but she had a fairly bristly moustache to make up for it. I couldn't believe it. I didn't even know the Peller lived in the house! I'd thought she was made up, like the Muffin Man.

'What the hell do you want?' the Peller said.

'Nothing,' I said. 'We're going. Sorry.'

I tried to go, but Miles wasn't budging.

'Do you live here?' Miles said.

'I do, yes,' she said. 'Some bastard has just broken all my windows and I'm waiting for the glazier to come.'

This didn't seem very witchy to me, but Miles was fascinated.

'Are you a witch? My friend says you're a witch,' he said. I nearly hit him. The Peller looked at me.

'Do you now?' she said to me. 'Well, I am not a witch, thank you! I'm a non-traditional healer. Haven't you ever heard of homeopathy?'

'Yes,' Miles said.

'Well, there you are then! Do I look like a witch to you?'

Neither of us answered, as there wasn't really much we could say. The rain started again, heavier than before since we no longer had the trees to shelter us.

'Oh, here we go again!' the Peller said. 'Where is that bloody glazier?'

She looked at us getting soggy in the cowslips. The sky was almost black with clouds.

'I wouldn't be surprised if a storm was coming,' she said. And the moment it was out of her mouth, a crack of thunder broke a few miles away.

'Typical,' she said. 'You'd better come in then. I don't want your parents coming round to complain after you get struck by lightning.'

We walked into the cottage. I expected to see a black cat curled up in front of a cauldron, but it looked like a completely ordinary house, with a fridge covered in photographs and dirty dishes in the sink. She had closed the green curtains to try to keep the wind out from the broken windows, and it cast a strange green light over the entire room.

'Do you want some squash?' she asked. 'Elderflower. I make it myself.'

She set two glasses in front of us.

'Where are your parents?' she asked. 'I'm not sure it's very clever to be walking in the woods without an adult, with all this . . . stuff going on.'

'You mean the murders?' Miles asked.

The Peller nodded.

221

'Those poor girls,' she said. 'Dreadful, dreadful.'

'They think they have the murderer,' I said. 'In jail. They've charged him.'

'George Brain?' the Peller laughed. 'If he's a murderer then I'll eat my hat. Man wouldn't hurt a fly.'

'You don't think it's him?' I asked. 'Everyone else does.'

'Well, it suits everyone else, doesn't it?' she said. 'The town can get back to normal. They can do their precious regatta. Ghastly Hoolhouse doesn't have to worry about George harping on in the quay. Mr Podmore can take over everything again. Yes, I'm sure it suits them all very well.'

I'd never heard a grown-up talk like this before, especially not in Fowey. She was even rude about Mr Podmore!

'I don't think George did it either,' I said proudly. 'And neither does Miles.'

'Well, I'm sure he'll go down for it, whatever the case,' the Peller sighed. 'Absolutely rotten. It's the reason I moved out of the town to here.'

'The murders?' I asked.

'No, not the murders!' she replied. 'I've lived here for years. I moved from all the sweetness and the good manners and Podmore sticking his nose into everyone's business. He doesn't own this cottage, thank goodness, or I'd be getting one of his letters to tell me to stop hanging my hag fingers in the doorway.'

'What are hag fingers?' Miles asked.

'Flint stones. Flint has very magical properties. My mother gave them to me, to protect against malevolent spirits, keep the home safe. Though they didn't really do much to stop my windows getting broken.'

I thought about the stones hanging on the ribbon outside, and something popped into my head.

'You know,' I said, 'the police found stones in the mouths of all the women. Well, two of them anyway.'

I didn't want to tell her that I'd filched the first one.

The Peller frowned.

'What do you mean?' she asked.

223

'The police think the murderer put stones in the girls' mouths,' I said. 'It's in all the papers.'

'I don't read the papers,' she said. 'What do the stones look like?'

I rummaged around in my satchel and brought out my stone. She took it from me and looked at it, turning it over. She opened the curtains so that she could get a better look, and the rain rushed into the room. A flash of lightning lit up her worried face.

'Where did you find this?' she asked.

Miles shook his head at me – only slightly, so that she couldn't see.

'I found it on the beach,' I said. 'It looked exactly like the one in the paper, so I picked it up for my fossil collection.'

'Strange. It's a sea urchin fossil,' the Peller said, running her fingers over it. 'My mother called them Thunder Stones. They're used as amulets. The Thunder Stone is supposed to bring safe passage to the wearer.'

'They obviously didn't work that well,' Miles snorted.

'No,' the Peller said. 'You're right. But what a very odd thing to do.'

'Pretty strange to kill someone in the first place, really,' I said.

'Yes,' the Peller agreed. 'But to then put a protective amulet with them. After killing them. That's shutting the door after the horse has bolted, I'd say!'

The Peller looked out at the rain and the lightning crackling across the sky.

'There was a story that we all grew up with around here,' she said, frowning. 'Now, what was it?'

She tapped the table with a long fingernail, trying to remember.

'There were sirens out in the ocean,' she said slowly as the memory crystallised. 'Do you know what sirens are?'

We didn't.

'They're like mermaids, only they aren't nice like mermaids. They sit on the rocks, singing strange songs, and bewitched sailors follow the sound and crash their ships into the rocks.'

'Pretty stupid of the sailors,' I said.

'Yes,' the Peller said. 'But they're hypnotised. They'll do anything to get to the sirens; they don't mind that their ships splinter and they drown. They need to be near the sirens.'

'And there were once sirens in Fowey?' I asked.

'According to the story,' the Peller said. 'But in the version I was told, there were some sailors who survived their shipwreck, and they were determined to get revenge on the sirens. So one night, they swam out into the sea. They could see a ship nearby, and knew that it would only be a matter of time until the sirens began to sing. Sure enough, the music started, but the men had heard it before and the magic no longer worked on them. To them, the singing sounded more like screaming, like death. The men swam silently to the rocks, cutting through the water like knives. The sirens were looking out at the ship, luring it closer; they didn't hear the men in the water behind them. Once they were close enough, the sailors grabbed the sirens and wound their own long hair around their necks, pulling it tighter until the glow from their siren skin faded and their silver eyes rolled back in their beautiful heads. Before they let them sink to the bottom of the sea, the men put stones on their tongues to make sure that, even in the afterlife, they never sang again.'

The Peller looked pale and shaky as she finished her story. She poured herself an elderflower cordial.

'That's just a fairy tale!' Miles said.

The Peller shrugged.

'George Brain was always talking about mermaids,' I said. 'He must have remembered the story too.'

'George,' the Peller sighed. 'Poor George. Maybe it was him. Who knows what people are capable of?'

'But he wouldn't be the only person who knew the story, would he?'

'No, I suppose not,' she said. 'Most of us would have heard it when we were children.'

'So the murderer, whoever they are,' I said, 'must come from Fowey, if they know the story.'

'Fowey or near enough. I don't see that anyone else would have heard it,' the Peller said. 'Unless the stones are just a coincidence.'

The stones weren't a coincidence, I was sure of it. And Miles and I had our first real clue in ages. The Peller didn't seem as happy about the discovery as we did. It fact, it seemed to make her sad, so once the rain had cleared a bit, Miles and I left.

We talked about George Brain the whole way back. Thinking about all the clues and what they meant. The main thing we thought, which seemed not to have occurred to Rottman, was that George was as thin and weak as a half-snapped twig, and blind drunk from the moment he woke up. How on earth would he be able to strangle someone? He would barely be able to catch them. I remembered him running from Rottman after the town meeting – he barely got a few feet before practically keeling over.

Miles and I are agreed that it cannot be George Brain. And that can only mean one thing: the murderer is still on the loose.

Everything smells like apples.

23

Apples

I am in bed still. I don't know how long I've been here.

Yesterday Miles and I snuck off to the tide pool again, since Mrs Tiggy-Winkle was still too weak to spend more than a few minutes out of bed.

When we got back to the hotel in the evening with our towels over our arms, Jean was shivering with excitement.

'You!' she said, pointing her bony finger at me. 'You're about to get it!'

Dorothea winced.

'What do you mean?' I said.

Aunt Maria trembled behind her desk. She wouldn't look at me.

Mrs Tiggy-Winkle stormed out of the parlour, apparently fully recovered. She somehow looked fatter than ever, in spite of days without food.

'Come away, Miles!' she screeched. 'Come away this instant!'

I looked pleadingly at Miles, but he shuffled over to his mother.

'You horrid little girl,' Mrs Tiggy-Winkle said. 'You horrid, horrid little girl.'

She steered Miles away, smoothing his jumper, jerking her head back to throw angry stares in my direction.

Winnie emerged from Uncle Frederick's study. She looked even happier than Jean.

'You'd better get in there,' she said. 'I wouldn't make him wait.'

What had I done? I had no idea. Did they know

about the Peller? But why would they mind that?
I hadn't done anything wrong.

I thought about bolting, but I knew Winnie
would come after me.

'Go on then!' Winnie said, shoving me forward.

I walked into the study and Winnie slammed
the door after me, leaving me alone with Uncle
Frederick. His study was dark and wood-panelled,
with thick velvet curtains, and it reeked of smoke
and his cinnamony aftershave. Like Christmas
gone wrong.

He sat at his desk, a sheen of sweat over his red
face. He stuck his tongue out to lick the sweat
off his upper lip.

What had I done?

He waited, staring at me, enjoying the moment.

'Have you had a nice day?' he asked.

'Yes, thank you, Uncle,' I whispered.

'Speak up,' he said.

'Yes, thank you, Uncle,' I repeated, louder.

'Do you know why you're here?' he asked,
as though he was talking to the village idiot,
stringing his words out.

'No,' I said.

'*No?* Can you guess?'

I shook my head.

Uncle Frederick tutted and wagged his finger at me.

'Naughty, naughty,' he sang.

He reached down into one of the drawers of his desk and pulled out Mrs Tiggy-Winkle's wiggly bottle. The one Miles had taken from her bag.

I'd forgotten about it. I had bloody forgotten about it.

I tried to look innocent. I stared at the bottle as though I'd never seen it before in my life.

'Do you know what this is?' he asked.

'No,' I said.

Uncle Frederick smiled. There was something stuck in his teeth.

'No? Are you sure?'

'Yes.'

'That is odd. Because Mrs Giffard noticed that it was missing this morning. Winnie thought you might have something to do with it, clever girl that she is, and she searched your room. Do you know where she found it?'

'No.'

'It was in your laundry basket. With all your dirty knickers.' He licked his lips again.

I stared at my shoes. I knew better than to say anything.

'Did you steal this bottle from Mrs Giffard?'

'No.'

'I don't believe you,' he said. 'Sit down.'

I sat in the chair opposite his. It had a velvet cushion on it.

He unscrewed the lid of the bottle and placed it in front of me.

'Well?' he said. 'Go on then.'

'What?' I asked.

'Well, you were planning on drinking it, weren't you? That's why you stole it.'

'No.'

'Yes, you did. You wanted to get all tipsy like the naughty girl that you are.' His face was getting redder and redder.

'No.'

'No?' he said. 'So I'm mistaken, am I? You just stole it because you liked the bottle?'

He slammed his fist down on the desk. I jumped. The liquid in the bottle shivered.

'Drink it,' he said.

I picked it up and took a sip. It was disgusting, like sweet, apple-flavoured mouthwash. I swallowed; it made my throat burn. I put the bottle down.

'There,' I said.

'What are you doing?' Uncle Frederick asked. 'I told you to drink it.'

'I did,' I choked.

Uncle Frederick got up and walked over to the big oak door. I heard the lock click into place. He sat back down. I picked the bottle back up.

'There we go,' he said. 'All of it.'

I held my nose to block the taste, but it kept rushing back up my throat. I swallowed it down. Halfway through, I put the bottle down again – I was certain I was going to be sick.

Uncle Frederick walked over to me and roughly put the bottle in my mouth; the glass crashed against my teeth. He tilted the bottle up, his other hand clamped to the back of my head to make sure I couldn't get away. I tried to swallow as fast as I could. Some of it went up my nose, and some dribbled out of my mouth and onto my clothes, but he didn't stop. I couldn't breathe. I started spluttering. He took the bottle away for a moment, a few inches left at the bottom. He waited while I recovered.

'Please, Uncle Frederick,' I said.

'Shut up,' he said.

He shoved the bottle into my mouth again. I could see the chunk in his teeth glistening.

After that I remember the stairs, and Aunt Maria's face. The lobby was empty except her. Again, she didn't look at me. I remember my bed sheets and the bath, but mostly I remember the toilet and the bathroom floor. I think Uncle Frederick came in . . . I think I remember – I don't know.

When I woke up, finally, I felt as though something had cracked me open. Like the snail on the ground with its shell smashed in. It was daytime, and Aunt Maria was in my room. I couldn't speak; I might as well have had a stone on my tongue.

Aunt Maria had a mop. The room and bathroom were spotless. Gleaming. I couldn't look at the dirty water in the bucket – I thought I might be sick again.

'I'm sorry,' she said. 'You shouldn't have stolen that bottle.'

She let herself out.

The hotel is full of Uncle Frederick's whistling. It is like nothing happened. Miles keeps on calling me a grumpy-guts. He doesn't know.

'I hope you gave her a good hiding,' Jean said to Uncle Frederick when I finally emerged in the dining room at teatime.

'Oh, she's learned her lesson,' Uncle Frederick said with a jolly smile. 'Haven't you?'

And I have.

24

Enemies

Miles has told Mrs Tiggy-Winkle that he hates me, and that he has a new friend in town called Bob. If Mrs Tiggy-Winkle is stupid enough to think that anyone our age is called Bob then she deserves to be lied to. Miles and I pretend to be enemies in the hotel, sticking our tongues out at each other and being snooty and rude, and then we meet up later in town.

Mrs Tiggy-Winkle and Jean have become the best of friends, united in their hatred for me, and sit together nattering in the parlour. Dorothea sits to one side, trying to join in the conversation, but Mrs Tiggy-Winkle and Jean just give little impatient sighs every time she opens her mouth, and then carry on their conversation. Jean likes to talk to Mrs Tiggy-Winkle about the fact that soon she'll need a qualified nurse, not just a companion, since she's getting on and her legs are getting worse. 'You'll have to go and bother someone else soon, Dorothea,' Jean says, with a wicked little chuckle. Jean knows that Dorothea doesn't have any money, or anywhere to live except for wherever Jean pays for, and she enjoys seeing Dorothea's stricken face when she reminds her how unsteady her position is. Dorothea looks like someone has sandpapered off a layer of her skin. The veins in her forehead twitch and her hands shake as she tries to do the crossword.

Miles thinks it's all Dorothea's fault, that she should have scarpered while she had the chance and got another job. I said he should try standing up to Jean, and that it's easier said than done.

The hotel is thinning out again. Most of the journalists have packed up and moved on to the next bloodthirsty crime; the rubberneckers have gone too, satisfied that the police have got their man. There are those in the town who are sceptical, like me and Miles and the Peller. The Flower twins whisper frantically, heads together, but daren't speak out for fear of displeasing Mr Podmore. When Miles and I went to the aquarium, Albert Fish seemed quite angry about it.

'It's not him,' Albert said. 'Poor George . . . Lord knows what will happen to him.'

'Who do you think it is?' I asked as Albert shook some flakes into the goldfish tank.

'Someone with a few screws loose, that's for certain,' Albert replied.

'He might still be out there,' I said. 'Plotting his next murder.'

'What's to say it's a "he"?' Albert said.

'Women don't strangle!' Miles said. 'Poisoning is what women do. They lack the brute strength for strangling.'

'Do they now?' Albert chuckled.

'Not if they use a rope,' I said. 'There's that lady in the *Who's Who* who strangled her husband with his favourite tie, remember? The one with the elephants on it.'

Miles seemed a bit annoyed that I'd corrected him.

'Maybe you two did it,' Albert said in a wobbly, spooky voice. 'You do know an awful lot about murder.'

I knew he was joking, but I was still quite flattered. We do know an awful lot about murder.

Miles and I went and bought a slice of bacon from the butcher and went crabbing off the end of the Yacht Club jetty. Technically you're only allowed there if you're a member, but the manager was hardly going to come over and tell a couple of kids to scram while all the snooty guests were having lunch and watching out of the window, so we just got the stink eye from a couple of waiters.

Miles doesn't like crabbing – he never catches anything; he's too impatient. He always pulls up his line too early or too fast, so even if there is a crab on the end of it, the thing will drop off before he has time to put it in the net. By the time Miles caught his first crab, my bucket already had six in it, crawling all over each other in the bottom.

Miles couldn't even hide his excitement when he finally saw the legs at the end of his line. It was only a little one, but it was better than nothing. He hauled the crab out and grabbed at it.

'Careful!' I said. 'It's caught in the net! You'll pull its legs off.'

Miles passed it over to me. I'm better at fiddly jobs than him, and the crab was wozzled up pretty good. As I untangled the net, I noticed something: it was a ring. Two of the crab's legs had got stuck through it.

'Look, Miles!' I said.

I jimmied the ring off carefully and plopped the crab into the bucket. The ring was gold, with a glittery multicoloured stone in it. I passed it over to Miles.

'It's an opal,' he said. 'They're supposed to be bad luck.'

He passed it back to me.

'Well, it obviously was bad luck if someone lost it in the sea,' I said, slipping it onto my finger. It was too big by miles, but it looked pretty.

'Can I see it again?' Miles said.

I stuck my hand out so that he could examine it.

'I've seen it before,' he said. 'In the paper. It belongs to one of the mermaids.'

We have started calling the victims 'the mermaids' so that people don't know what we're talking about.

'Which one?' I said.

'Belle Gunness,' he said.

This gave me a thrill. The mermaid's ring! I liked it even more now.

'Don't wear it,' he said. 'Someone might notice. Put it in your satchel.'

I didn't want to, but he had a point. I put it in the special pocket, with the Thunder Stone.

'Do you think the murderer put her in the water here then?' I asked.

'The crab could have walked from anywhere, couldn't it?' he said.

'I guess the Yacht Club wouldn't be the best place to throw a body in the water,' I said. 'Someone might notice.'

We looked up at the Yacht Club veranda. Mayor Hoolhouse was having lunch with his wife, both of them with matching sherbet-orange jumpers tied around their shoulders and occasionally glaring at us, annoyed that we'd ruined their precious view. On the table next door was Peter Queen, eating alone, staring out at the water.

When we walked back to the centre of town, there was a crowd outside the Fowey Museum.

'What's going on?' I asked Albert Fish, who had stepped out of the aquarium to see what the ruckus was.

'Someone wrote something on the typewriter,' he said.

Inside the museum, along with the taxidermy, ships in bottles and military uniforms, is a typewriter that belonged to Sir Arthur Quiller-Couch. He was the most famous writer in Fowey until Daphne du Maurier came along and stole his thunder. His typewriter always has fresh paper on it, and anyone who goes to the museum can type something if they like. I've always liked writing rude things or made-up gossip from the town, but mostly people write their names and the date that they visited the museum.

The man who curates the museum, Thomas Orrock, claims to be a descendent of the original Podmore from centuries ago. He always wears the Podmore family signet ring, even though Mr Podmore has written to him millions of times asking him to stop. He stood outside the museum, clutching a bit of typewriter paper. He was wearing a pair of woolly gloves, which looked rather bonkers with his summer outfit.

'It's just not cricket!' he kept on saying.

Eventually PC Nodder arrived. 'What is it, Mr Orrock?' he asked, swinging back and forth on his shiny shoes in an official manner.

'Where's DCI Rottman?' Orrock said. 'I need a proper policeman.'

PC Nodder looked like he might thump Mr Orrock.

'I am a proper policeman, thank you very much,' Nodder spluttered. 'DCI Rottman has gone back to London. I'm in charge again, you'll all be pleased to hear.'

Someone in the crowd groaned. Nodder ignored it.

'Let's have a look at this, please,' he said, snatching the paper from Thomas Orrock's hands.

'Shouldn't you be using gloves?' Thomas Orrock said. 'What if there are fingerprints?'

'No time for gloves, Mr Orrock,' PC Nodder said, reading the message.

PC Nodder laughed.

'Well,' he said. 'This is clearly a joke. I'm afraid someone is playing a prank on you. We have apprehended the murderer, as you well know. George Brain is the man. Stacks of evidence against him.'

'What does it say?' I asked.

'Just someone making trouble,' Nodder said. He handed the paper back to Orrock.

'Shouldn't you take it?' Orrock said. 'As evidence?'

'Evidence of what? Someone having a laugh?' Nodder addressed the crowd now. 'It seems Mr Orrock has got a bit excited over nothing. Move along, everyone. No need to clog the thoroughfare.'

People started moving off, a bit disappointed, and those who hung around got glared at by Nodder. 'Back to work now, please,' he said pointedly to the last stragglers.

Miles and I walked off and waited for a bit, and once Nodder had gone, we circled back to the museum.

Thomas Orrock was sitting at his desk, which was piled high with Quiller-Couch and Du Maurier books, and old medals from the war. He was looking at the paper, which was a bit crumpled from Nodder grabbing it.

'I can't understand it,' he said. 'I've been in here all day. I didn't hear the typewriter – at least, I don't think I did. It's been busy the past few days.'

'What does it say?' I asked.

He passed me the paper. I showed it to Miles. Three words:

I DID IT.

'Is that all it says?' I asked.

Thomas Orrock nodded.

'Do you remember who's been in here?' I said.

'I'm not sure,' he said. 'I've been cataloguing all the old books, and the museum has been so busy with all the murders. I usually notice if someone has written on the typewriter, though, because I have to check it for swear words. We had some problems a couple of years ago with someone writing obscenities on it.'

'What's this?' Miles asked. There was a large leather ledger open on the top of a glass cabinet of curiosities.

'Oh!' Orrock said. 'You clever thing! The guest book!'

Orrock put his glasses on. He rushed over to the ledger and ran his finger down the names.

'Richard Speck and family . . . Herefordshire. Yes! I remember them, very nice, brought in a dog. Don't think it would be them. Bertie Manton . . . Oxford . . . oh, well, he was only about your age. Not him.'

He ran through a couple of names and addresses of people he didn't remember. Then his finger stopped.

'How odd,' he said. 'What a strange name. And they haven't left an address.'

Miles and I leaned in to look. The writing was tiny, the letters all crammed together, even though there was plenty of space in the line:

Mr Kipper.

I glanced at Miles. Mr Kipper was in our murder book. Miles didn't look like he remembered.

'Do you remember Mr Kipper?' Miles said.

Orrock rubbed his face. 'I'm afraid I don't,' he said.

'I suppose I should call PC Nodder back,' Thomas Orrock said. 'My ancestors the Podmores would not want me to let this man go free.'

'Good luck with getting Nodder to listen to you,' I said.

After Miles and I left, I reminded him about the Mr Kipper in our book.

'Of course I remember,' Miles said.

'It's a weird coincidence, isn't it?' I asked.

Miles sighed.

'You can be awfully thick sometimes, can't you?' he said.

It was only when we got back to the hotel that I realised what he meant.

25

Carnival Queen

Regatta Week starts next week, and every window and doorknob and letterbox in the town is sparkling. The Union flags have been freshly laundered and strung up all over the Town Hall, and the pubs are rolling in extra barrels to cope with the visitors. Mayor Hoolhouse is determined that it will be the best regatta ever, to try to distance the town from all the murders. I'm not really sure that there is enough confetti in the world to make people forget about girls being strangled all over the place, but Hoolhouse is dedicated to making it work. He stalks around the place, manically checking that everything looks spick and span, and he has removed all the flowers and letters tied to the railings on the quay in memory of the victims. He says that a regatta is no time to be glum, and if the girls' families are cross about it then maybe they should go elsewhere for a few days.

The only thing Hoolhouse hasn't done is select this year's Carnival Queen. There was a bit of a problem surrounding this, since two of the girls who had been killed were former Queens, and even Mrs Hoolhouse seemed to think it might be a bit insensitive to go through with it. Mayor Hoolhouse wasn't having any of it – he wants the parade to be just as it has always been, and if that means having a girl dressed as a fairy carted around behind a tinsel-covered tractor then he'll bloody well have it.

'I think it's downright sinister,' Jean said to Mrs Tiggy-Winkle in the parlour. 'A child with a face full of make-up being paraded around. It's indecent!'

252

Winnie was dusting off the ornaments on top of the mantelpiece and bristled a bit at this.

'I agree, Jean,' Mrs Tiggy-Winkle said. 'It's not proper.'

Miles was sitting next to his mother, pretending to ignore me while I flipped through the *Who's Who*. As far as Mrs Tiggy-Winkle is concerned, we are still enemies.

'It's tradition!' Winnie said. 'I don't see what's wrong with it. I was Carnival Queen myself.'

Miles and I rolled our eyes at each other.

Jean pursed her lips.

'Yes, Winnie, dear,' she said. 'But that was a long time ago. Things are different now.'

'It wasn't that long ago!' Winnie said.

'Maybe not,' Jean said. 'But we only need to look at what has happened in the town this summer. Who knows what perverts will be lurking in the crowd?'

'Jean,' Dorothea said, 'it's just a parade. I'm sure there won't be any perverts.'

'Oh, what would you know, Dorothea?' Jean snapped. 'You don't know what men are like. They're animals.'

'Quite right,' Mrs Tiggy-Winkle said, squeezing Miles protectively. 'You're not like that, are you, Milesy?'

'No, Mother,' Miles said.

'No.' Mrs Tiggy-Winkle beamed at Jean. 'He's a good little boy.'

'Of course he is,' Jean smiled back. 'For now, but you'd be surprised, Mrs Giffard, what goes on in the minds of these young boys. You read all sorts of chilling things in the papers, don't you? Boys who just go out and do terrible things. Monsters. Their mothers never know what's going on.'

'Oh, I'm sure they do really,' Mrs Tiggywinkle said. 'A mother always knows.'

'I'm not so sure about that, Mrs Giffard,' Jean answered in her most goading voice, looking at Miles. 'Not so sure at all.'

Mrs Tiggy-Winkle gave Jean a tight smile.

'I think I've had enough of this stuffy parlour,' Mrs Tiggy-Winkle said. 'It's giving me a headache.'

She lumbered up. 'Come on, Miles,' she said.

After they walked out, Dorothea couldn't help but allow herself a small smile.

'She dotes on that boy,' Jean said. 'It's not healthy!'

Miles snuck into my room later.

'It looks like your mother and Jean had a bit of a run-in,' I said.

'She was furious,' Miles said. 'Says she's never speaking to Jean again.'

'She can try,' I said.

I'd filched some lipstick from the chemist earlier and had been trying it on before Miles came in.

'You look like the Carnival Queen,' he said, 'with all that muck on your face.'

'I was only seeing what it looked like,' I said. 'As a joke.'

I wiped it off quickly with the corner of the bed sheet. It looked like a blood smear.

Miles tapped his fingers on his knees, studying me.

'You know what *would* be a good joke?' he said.

'What?' I asked.

'If you entered to be the Carnival Queen.'

'Me?' I said. 'Don't be an idiot!'

'Why not?' he said. 'You're pretty enough, and you're the right age.'

Pretty! I thought.

'The whole thing is stupid,' I said. 'Prancing around like a fairy. And they wouldn't pick me anyway.'

'They might!' he said. 'If you did yourself up with all that lip gunk and put on a dress.'

'They wouldn't.'

'And if they did, you could get up on the float and do something.'

'Like what?'

'Like, I don't know, give the whole town the finger or throw stink bombs.'

'Uncle Frederick would kill me.'

'Think of how annoyed Winnie would be if you got it.'

That swung it. The idea of Winnie's furious face as I rode around wearing her tiara, with everyone throwing flowers on me.

I went to sleep, with Miles sleeping top to toe, dreaming of myself on the glittery throne, wearing a beautiful white dress and with everyone cheering my name. I could see Miles in the crowd, gazing at me and noticing how pretty everyone thought I was.

26

The Fish

I spent hours on my make-up for the choosing of the Queen. I wanted to get it absolutely right, so I tore out a page from one of the magazines in the parlour and asked Aunt Maria if I could borrow some of her make-up. She was so surprised when I told her what it was for that she agreed, and lent me a stripy bag, which smelled like it hadn't been opened for a while.

'I don't wear make-up much any more,' Aunt Marie said as she handed the bag over.

'Frederick says it does me no favours.'

She hesitated.

'Make sure he doesn't see you on the way out,' she said. 'I'm not sure he'd like it.'

I started with a thick layer of browny-pink-coloured liquid all over my face, to give myself the 'healthy glow' the magazine suggested, and then applied some blusher. The magazine said you had to smile to find 'the apple of your cheeks', and I thought I looked a bit mad in the mirror doing it, but the bright-pink circles came out quite well because of it and definitely made me look 'in the first flush of love'. I tried to follow the eye routine, but that didn't work quite so well – the black pencil kept smudging and the mascara made all my eyelashes stick together, but the purple eyeshadow certainly made my eyes 'the feature' of my face, and the effect was quite dramatic, which is what the magazine had suggested. I used a red lipstick and drew the outline of my lips over the top. The magazine had said to use a 'lip pencil', but the only pencil in the bag was the eye one, so I just used that. It looked pretty much the same as the picture anyway – even better, I thought. I finished by painting on a beauty spot – the magazine hadn't suggested that, but I thought it would add an air of glamour, so I put it just above my lip.

When I stood back and looked, my face really did look different. My hair had grown out a bit, slightly unevenly, but there wasn't really much I could do with that. It would look fine with the crown on it anyway. I didn't have a dress either, but I thought Aunt Maria would have to buy me one if I was Carnival Queen, so it didn't really matter if I didn't have one now. Better to save it for later for maximum impact.

I was meeting Miles in the town as usual, and had to slip out through the kitchen so Uncle Frederick didn't see.

'*Mon Dieu!*' Joseph said as I ran past him. 'What have you done to your face, *soupçon*?'

I didn't have time to stop – I didn't want to miss the beginning of the ceremony – and ran all the way down to the quay.

Mayor Hoolhouse was wearing a special striped pink suit for the occasion, and had a clipboard with the names of all the girls who were entering written on it. Miles had put my name down. A few people turned to look as I walked through the crowd – I was 'turning heads', which was exactly what the magazine had said would happen!

'Good Lord,' Mayor Hoolhouse said when I walked up to him to check in. 'Is this a joke?'

'No,' I said. I felt a bit self-conscious now.

Mayor Hoolhouse gave a little irritated sigh.

'Right then,' he said, ticking me off his list. 'Get up on the wall with the rest of them.'

All of the girls were already lined up on the wall in their best kit. There were eight of us, including me. Mary Pearcey was there, wearing one of her frothy pink dresses and little diamond stud earrings, and socks with a frill around the top. She looked at me with a bit of a startled face, so I pushed her to one side and climbed up into the best position in the middle. I did my best pose, hands on hips, and gave my biggest smile.

I could see that I was getting most of the attention, which was annoying the other girls a bit. People were whispering and pointing at me. Even Miles was staring. We had to wait for Mayor Hoolhouse to pick the judge.

The judge of the queen contest is always a stranger, so they can't be biased. It can't be someone who lives in the town because they'd always be picking their daughter or niece or goddaughter.

Mayor Hoolhouse hunted through the crowd. 'I know you,' he said jovially, looking at faces. 'And you!' Finally he got to someone he hadn't seen before. 'What about you, sir?' Hoolhouse said. 'Will you judge these little girls for us?'

The man looked embarrassed. He obviously hadn't understood how the thing worked.

'Can't someone else do it?' he said. 'I don't think I'm qualified.'

Hoolhouse smiled impatiently. 'Oh, you'll do,' he said. 'Don't you worry!'

Hoolhouse tried to guide the man to the front.

'I'd really rather not,' the man hissed.

Hoolhouse grinned at the crowd. 'Just do it!' he said through his teeth.

There was some resistance from the man, but eventually Hoolhouse dragged him up to the front.

The man was quite sweaty, and was wearing a tweed jacket on one of the hottest days of the year.

'Can you tell us your name? And where you are from?' Hoolhouse said, like a game-show host.

'My name is Brian,' the man replied, with no enthusiasm. 'And I'm from Par.'

'Par?' Hoolhouse said, annoyed. 'That's only down the road. Oh well, never mind!'

Hoolhouse waved an arm in our direction.

'All you have to do is choose our Carnival Queen for the Regatta Parade, and two handmaidens to help her onto the float,' Hoolhouse said.

'How old are these girls?' Brian said, squinting up at us.

'Never mind that,' Hoolhouse said. 'We haven't got all day. Just pick one!'

Brian turned to study us. He walked up and down the wall a few times. We all batted our eyelashes and pointed our toes. He stopped in front of me and Mary. Mary dipped into a little curtsey. I didn't want to be outdone, so I copied her, but I hadn't got my balance quite, so I very nearly wobbled off the wall. The crowd gasped, and Brian put out his hand to steady me.

'Right!' Hoolhouse said. 'Who is it to be?'

I held my breath; I felt sure he was going to point at me. And he did.

'This girl here . . .' he said – I nearly screamed – 'for handmaiden.'

I wanted to punch him. HANDMAIDEN? WHAT A SWIZZ!

He pointed to another girl, with dark curly hair, and made her the second handmaiden.

'And the Queen?' Hoolhouse asked.

The man thought for a while, and finally pointed at Mary. The crowd cheered.

'That, I believe . . .' Hoolhouse said, consulting his clipboard, 'is Mary Pearcey! Mary is a keen swimmer and is spending her summer holiday here in Fowey.'

'Come on, Mary!' Mr Pearcey shouted, punching the air. Mary blushed and gave another little curtsey, to much whooping.

I got off the wall. Miles walked up to me. I felt like my face had been shoved in a fire, I was so red.

'Well done,' Miles said. 'Handmaiden.'

'I didn't want to be handmaiden,' I said. 'I wanted to be the Queen!'

Miles laughed. 'I thought you didn't care!'

'I don't care. It's just stupid, that's all.'

'Well, maybe you should have looked in the mirror before you came down,' Miles said. 'You look like a clown.'

Mary sashayed up to us. 'Hi, Miles,' she said, ignoring me.

'Congratulations, Mary,' Miles said.

'Thank you,' she said. 'Daddy is buying me a new white dress for it. And a necklace.'

She turned to me.

'You have to get a matching dress too,' she said. 'We all have to be matching. And you have to do something about your hair, because it looks silly.'

I turned on my heel and walked off. I didn't want to look at her stupid face for another second. It was so unfair! I hadn't even wanted to do the stupid thing in the first place. Miles had made me do it. And now Mary was going to be the Queen, and I was going to have to stand behind her in a stupid white dress, and Miles would be looking at her instead of me.

I went into the aquarium, the first place I could think of. Albert wasn't there. I thought about sticking my hand in the eel tank. That would show everyone, if I came out all bleeding with my hand bitten off. Then no one would be talking about stupid Mary any more. But the eels weren't in the tank; there was nothing in the tank, not even water. Albert must have been halfway through cleaning it, because there were bottles of bleach on the side and a big scrubbing brush. I looked at the fish tank. That was how I felt too: cold and floating and stuck behind glass.

The thing is, I didn't really even know I was doing it.

But then it was done and all the fish were dead.

But then Albert really shouldn't have left the bleach lying around, should he? If he didn't want something like that to happen.

27

News in the Paper

Albert Fish has closed the aquarium; he says there's no point keeping it open, after someone did something like that. He doesn't know it was me. I don't even think it was me, really – it seems so unlikely now I almost feel like I imagined the whole thing.

Aunt Maria agreed to buy me a dress for the regatta float, since I have to be up there standing behind Mary. It is thin white cotton, with lace around the top. Aunt Maria says I have to wear a vest with it in case anyone can see through it, because Jean has made her terrified about perverts.

Uncle Frederick is pleased that I'm in the parade. He says it's the sort of thing normal girls my age should be doing and even forked out for some new white plimsoles that I can wear with the dress.

I'm trying to get excited about it, but every time I do I think of how I have to stand behind Mary, and how everyone keeps going on about how pretty she is and what a fine Queen she'll make. She doesn't even live here! She's only here on holiday. Mrs Hoolhouse is in charge of making sure everything is just so, and has roped Mary, me and the other girl, Martha, into decorating the float and the Carnival Queen banner.

Miles keeps teasing me about how much I want to be Queen, and Mary orders me around every time we do a practice procession, telling me how to wave and how to smile.

I went into Queen's Sweetshop to buy some more pebble sweets to cheer myself up after one of Mary's boring lectures about posture, and Peter Queen was reading the paper. He looked a bit peaky and didn't respond even when I called his name a few times. I threw a sweet at him and he looked up.

'Oh,' he said faintly. 'It's you.'

He took my money for the sweets.

'What's in the paper?' I asked.

He looked back down at the front page.

'It's George Brain,' he said. 'He's dead.'

According to the paper, George Brain had hanged himself with a bed sheet in his police cell.

Everyone at the hotel seems to think that this proves George did it, but now the papers are starting to say that George had an alibi for one of the murders, and maybe he didn't do it after all.

'They're just stirring up trouble,' said Jean, poring over the papers in the lobby. 'Selling more papers. And if it wasn't him, who was it? A load of tosh.'

'Quite right, Jean!' Uncle Frederick said. 'Absolute rubbish. George was never right in the head, and this just shows it.'

'I'm glad he hanged himself,' said Winnie. 'Saves the taxpayer money, doesn't it?'

'That it does, Winnie,' Uncle Frederick agreed. 'That it does.'

Miles is keen to get a boat and go rowing along the coast this weekend; he says he's bored of the town. There's a little boat that the hotel has for guests, but I said we'd never be allowed to take it by ourselves. 'You're getting so wet,' Miles said. 'We can just take it, can't we? We don't need to ask.'

He wants to go up and have a poke around in the old World War Two pillbox. Mary overheard us talking about it in town.

'Can I come too?' she asked.

'It's quite a small boat,' I said. 'I don't think we'll all fit.'

'I'm sure we could fit one more in,' Miles said. 'Bring some proper shoes, though, or you won't be able to climb up with us.'

'I've got some trainers.'

Miles leaned in towards Mary and murmured, 'And don't tell your father where we're going.'

'Why not?' Mary giggled.

'Because we're not supposed to take the boat, silly.'

Mary zipped her mouth shut with her fingers.

I was annoyed on our walk back up to the hotel.

'Why did you have to ask Mary?' I said.

'Just because you're jealous that she's the Carnival Queen,' he said.

'No, I'm not! She's a drip, that's all. And she'll whinge the whole day.'

'Well, we're not going to be here much longer, are we?' he said. 'So there's no point in fighting.'

He knows I don't like to talk about this.

Regatta Week is the last week of the summer holidays, and we both have to go home on Sunday. I usually look forward to going back to Granny's, because it means I can go and knock on Mr West's door and tell him all about my summer, but I'm dreading it this year. I don't even mind about Mr West any more really, and haven't written him any letters like I usually do.

There isn't a chance in the world that Mrs Tiggy-Winkle will let Miles see me once we get home, and Miles doesn't seem half as worried about it as I do, so I've been pretending that I don't mind either, but I think he knows I do mind because he keeps on teasing me about it.

Joseph says this will be his last year cooking in the hotel, and that the town has changed since all the girls went missing. He's going to work in London in a Greek restaurant. I'm going to miss him too, but at least I can tell him that, because he is French and doesn't mind talking about his feelings. The other night he made me a special pineapple mousse.

'You should spend your summer in another place next year,' he said.

'I don't have much choice, do I?' I said.

'Your uncle,' Joseph said. 'You know, I notice. He is not kind to you.'

I stopped eating the mousse; suddenly I didn't want it any more.

'He's all right,' I said.

'No, *soupçon*,' he said.

It was all very well for Joseph to feel sorry for me, but where did he think I could go instead?

Granny won't take me on her trip, and I can hardly spend the summer by myself.

'I'm fine, Joseph,' I said, a bit more crossly than I meant to.

Joseph lit another cigarette and looked at the burning tip.

'You'll understand when you grow up,' he said.

'I am grown up,' I said.

28

The Pillbox

We went on our boat trip today.

Mary came up to the hotel, and we all met down at the bottom of the cliff steps. Mrs Tiggy-Winkle thinks Miles has gone on a day trip with 'Bob's' family. I don't know why she doesn't suspect anything, since she's never even met Bob, but Miles says she'll believe anything he tells her.

The boat was small, with two wooden slats to sit on and a puddle of water at the bottom. The blue paint was flaking, and the letters of its name *Manderley* were so faint you could hardly read them.

Mary pouted. 'It doesn't look very safe,' she said. 'And we'll get our shoes all wet.'

'Don't come then, if you mind about your shoes,' I snapped.

Mary scowled at me.

'You can sit next to me, Mary,' Miles said. 'And put your feet up on the side so your shoes stay dry.'

It annoyed me that Miles was paying so much attention to Mary, so I stomped onto the boat, getting my shoes wet on purpose to show that I didn't mind a bit of water on my feet.

Mary snuggled in next to Miles, but then he made her move and sit next to me when he realised that he wouldn't be able to row with her in the way. She sat down ungraciously next to me, pulling her legs away dramatically so that they didn't touch mine.

Mary talked about the carnival non-stop in the boat, until I had to grind my teeth to stop myself from telling her to shut up. Miles rowed us round down to the beach near St Catherine's point. There are so many boats around during Regatta Week that no one looked twice at us – a few other sailors even waved.

The beach was deserted – it's quite pebbly and grey, and not really a popular spot, but we thought we might be able to find some fish in the rock pools and have our picnic nearby. There was a dead sheep lying on its back with its legs poker straight in the air. Sometimes they fall off the cliffs.

'Yuck!' Mary said as Miles and I approached. 'It stinks!'

It must have been there for a while, because it was covered in flies, which flew into the air in a cloud when Miles poked it with a stick.

'Don't, Miles!' Mary said. 'It's disgusting!'

I turned to Mary.

'Dare you to touch it,' I said.

'Eugh! No!' Mary said.

'Come on, Mary,' Miles said. 'A dare's a dare, isn't it?'

Mary was stuck. She didn't want to disappoint Miles.

She hovered near it, holding her nose.

'You have to touch it for a couple of seconds,' I said. 'Otherwise it doesn't count.'

Mary put her hand out, closing her eyes. She touched the wool and her hand shot back.

'Doesn't count!' Miles said.

Mary took a deep breath and put her hand back on the sheep's side, whimpering.

'One . . .' I said, as slowly as I could. 'Two . . . Three!'

Mary ran over to the sea and plunged her hand in, not minding now that her feet were wet. Miles and I were on the ground, laughing.

Mary came back, drying her hands on her skirt.

'If you think it's so funny, why don't you do it then?' she asked.

I walked over to the sheep and put my hand on its stomach. I didn't mind touching dead things after Fucko the cat. I stroked the sheep a bit, just to rub it in. Mary shrugged.

'Let's have the picnic,' she said. 'I'm hungry.'

Mary had brought her own lunch – crab sandwiches and a slice of cake – but she would only share the cake with Miles. I had to make do with my pebble sweets.

We spent the afternoon swimming and rock pooling. There were limpets on the rocks, stuck fast, and I tried for ages to prise one off with an old mussel shell, but it wouldn't let go.

Mary spent the whole time trying to get Miles's attention, splashing him in the water and running away so he would catch her. I pretended not to care and put sand in her shoes while they were swimming. When she got back from the sea, she didn't even say anything; she just poured the sand out and rolled her eyes at Miles.

I sunbathed, wanting to get a tan to look good in my white dress for the procession the next day. Mary was already golden and kept shoving her arm against mine to show me what a better colour she was.

Finally, the evening began to set in and the sea started to creep towards us.

'We should go up to the pillbox,' Miles said. 'Before it gets too dark.'

To get there, we had to row up beneath it and tie the boat to the bottom of the iron stepladder that was set into the rock face. Mary looked up.

'I don't like heights,' she said. 'Can't I wait here?'

'The whole point of today was to come to the pillbox, Mary,' Miles said. 'Don't be a baby about it.'

'Yeah, Mary,' I said.

'But what if I fall?' she said.

'You won't fall,' Miles said. 'You go first, and I'll follow behind.'

Mary put her foot on the first step. It did look a bit precarious. She looked back at us nervously.

'Just don't look down,' Miles said. 'You'll be fine.'

Mary wobbled up slowly, making sure both feet were on each step before she set off again. Miles started after her, with me going last.

It took us a while to get up to the pillbox, since Mary was such a scaredy-cat about the whole thing. It looked as though no one had been up there for decades. Huge nettles had grown up around the squat concrete box, and we had to be careful not to get our bare legs stung. In the old days there would have been a path up onto the cliff walk, but the nettles and gorse and brambles had now made that impossible.

'Shall we go in?' Miles asked.

'There might be someone in there,' Mary said, uncertain.

'Who?' Miles asked. 'Don't be silly.'

Miles ducked into the pillbox, and I went in after him. It was incredibly dark, just a stone room with two slits for windows. Someone had graffitied the inside a bit, and there were old beer cans on the floor.

Mary came in, holding herself so that she didn't brush past any cobwebs. It was freezing cold and stank of damp. Miles peered out of the window. 'They would have shot people from up here,' he said.

'It's creepy,' Mary said.

'That's because it's haunted by all the soldiers who died up here,' I said.

Mary clung onto Miles. 'Can we go back?' she said.

'In a minute,' Miles said.

The patches of light from the window were getting fainter, and it was hard to see.

'How long do you think you could stay in here by yourself?' Miles asked.

'I could stay here all night,' I said. 'I'm not scared of a few ghosts.'

'I don't like the dark,' Mary said.

'Do you think you could stay in here for a full minute, Mary?' Miles said.

'No way,' Mary said.

'Really? Not even for me?' Miles asked, putting on a soppy voice. I looked away. I didn't understand why Miles was paying so much attention to Mary.

Mary wavered, looking around the pillbox.

'A minute?' she said.

'Yes,' Miles answered.

'And would you wait outside the whole time?' Mary asked. 'In case I screamed?'

'Yep,' Miles answered.

'Okay,' Mary said. 'I'll do it if you give me a kiss.'

I wanted to be sick. Asking for a kiss! I felt sure Miles would laugh at her, but he didn't.

'All right,' he said.

She closed her eyes and tilted her head up, and Miles dipped down and kissed her full on the lips. I couldn't stop watching, and wanted to go over and pull them apart, but I couldn't move. I thought I might burst into tears. Finally Miles pulled away, and Mary laughed. I felt sure she was laughing at me.

'One minute,' Miles said.

We left her inside the pillbox. I couldn't even look at Miles I was so cross. I was about to hit him when he grabbed my hand. He put his fingers to his lips and guided me to the stepladder. He pointed downwards.

Suddenly I realised what he was doing. It was a trick! He had only kissed her for a trick! I thought I might explode with happiness. We climbed down the ladder as quick as a flash and leapt into the boat. Miles untied the rope just as we heard Mary calling out for him. He rowed us into a dip in the rocks so we could just see Mary as she looked around to find us. She thought we were hiding behind the pillbox.

I giggled, and Miles put his hand over my mouth. He was watching, breathless.

'Miles!' Mary called. 'Stop it!' She walked around the pillbox a few times, her voice getting higher and louder each time.

'This isn't funny,' she said uncertainly. 'I know you're hiding.'

She was starting to panic.

'Where are you?' she said. She walked down to the stepladder and stood staring at the patch of water where the boat had been.

'No!' she cried out. 'No!'

We ducked down when she turned her head in our direction. She didn't see us.

'Where are you?' she yelled. 'Come back!'

She started pacing around, like a spider stuck in a glass. Boatless. Friendless. There was no way out. She looked down at the water below her, and she knew she couldn't swim the whole way round the bay. She turned and looked up the hill, overgrown with brambles and nettles and dangerously steep.

'Help!' she called. 'Help!'

The call didn't go very far, with the wind blowing and the sea beneath her.

She began to cry – not little tears, but great big sobs. She was certain we had left her.

It was getting dark. Soon Mary wouldn't be able to see two feet in front of her. She looked up the hill again. She was thinking, could she run through the nettles? She could make it up to the cliff walk maybe, if she tried.

'Should we tell her?' I whispered.

'Wait a bit,' Miles whispered back, his eyes never leaving Mary's shaking body.

Mary sniffled again and called out Miles's name. He didn't respond. We watched her for a few minutes as she tried to find a path through the thicket. There was none.

'Miles,' I said, 'we'll get into trouble.' I hated Mary, but I didn't really fancy Mr Pearcey finding out.

'Wait,' he said, never taking his eyes away from Mary. She was the ghost in the pillbox now.

Mary began to walk into the nettles, crying as she tried to elbow her way through. They were as high as her face. She put her arms in front of her to try to protect herself, but both Miles and I could see that there wasn't much chance of that. Every time she tried to push the nettles out of the way they snapped back and whipped at her. The crying had stopped; she was moaning now, whimpering.

'Miles,' I said again, pulling at his sleeve.

'All right,' he said.

He stood up on the boat. 'MARY!' he called. Mary had half disappeared into the nettles. She turned back. She was still panicking – she didn't know what was going on.

'What are you doing?' he called.

Mary was shaking like a kicked dog. She disentangled herself from the nettles and brambles and walked slowly up to the cliff. She could hardly look at us. Even from where I was sitting, with the darkness setting in, I could see marks all over her arms and legs.

'Mary!' Miles said, his voice full of concern. 'What's going on?'

'Why did you go?' she asked, her voice catching on thick sobs.

'The rope got loose, the boat was floating away!' Miles said. 'We had to get it and then we got caught on the tide. It took us a bit of time to row back!'

Mary didn't look like she believed him.

'Why didn't you answer?' she asked. 'When I called for help.'

'We did!' I said. 'Didn't you hear us?'

'I'm coming up,' Miles said, and started up the ladder.

Mary flinched and stepped away from the edge of the cliff, frightened.

I watched jealously as Miles gave her a hug when he reached the top. She was confused – she wanted to believe him.

Miles looked at her scratches and stings sympathetically.

'I thought you'd gone!' she cried. 'I thought you'd left me here!'

'Why would we do that?' Miles said. 'Come on, let's get down into the boat before it's too dark to see.'

It took Mary an age to get down into the boat she was shaking so much.

Up close, I could see that her face was already swelling from the stings. Her body was covered in a pink rash and white pimples. Miles took off his jumper and gave it to her, cooing and fussing over her. Even though she was in agony, she couldn't help but love the attention and began trembling again to get Miles to give her another hug.

'I can't believe you thought we'd left you,' he said.

'I didn't know,' Mary said. 'I thought you had.'

We rowed towards the hotel. I was starting to get a bit nervous about how we would explain it all, especially since we weren't supposed to be in the boat, and Miles and I weren't even supposed to be friends. It seemed as though Miles was thinking the same thing, because he said, 'You won't tell you father what happened, will you?'

Mary didn't respond.

'Because, you know we'd all get into a lot of trouble if anyone knew about the boat.'

He squeezed her hand.

'You won't tell?'

Mary kept quiet.

When we got back to the hotel, Miles and Mary went in first, and I hung around a bit outside so no one would see us all together.

When I finally walked into the lobby everyone was making a big old fuss over Mary while they waited for Mr Pearcey to arrive. Aunt Maria had got the first-aid kit out and Winnie had run off to fetch Mary a hot chocolate. Mary looked even worse in the light of the lobby, pink and raw as a prawn and her face was swelling up an absolute treat. Jean was saying loudly to Mrs Tiggy-Winkle that Mary should go to the hospital, because she had heard of people who had died from nettle stings before and the bramble scratches might go septic. I secretly wished they would. Mary clung onto Miles throughout, not letting him leave her side.

When Mr Pearcey arrived he was in an absolute frenzy.

'What happened?' he shouted at Miles, kneeling down to look at Mary.

'She tripped and fell in a nettle bush,' Miles said.

'Is this true, Mary?' Mr Pearcey asked.

Mary bit her lip. Miles and I waited, holding our breath.

'Yes, Daddy,' Mary said. 'Miles helped me. He gave me his jumper.'

'Oh, Miles!' Mrs Tiggy-Winkle said. 'You are a good boy!'

Mr Pearcey turned to shake Miles's hand.

'Thank you,' he said. 'Thank goodness you were there.'

'No problem at all, sir,' Miles said in his most respectful, high, polite voice.

Miles knocked on my door in the middle of the night, like he always did.

'Well?' he said, after I let him in.

'Well, what?' I said.

'Aren't you going to thank me?'

'For what? For nearly getting us both into the biggest trouble ever?'

'No, you idiot,' Miles said. 'For the carnival.'

I felt a bit thick. I wasn't really sure what he was on about.

'You wanted to be Carnival Queen, didn't you?'

'Not really,' I said, as snootily as I could.

'Well, you kept banging on about it. And I don't think Mary is going to be able to get on the float with her face swollen up like a sack of potatoes, is she?'

He grinned.

'You did it on purpose . . .' I said.

'You'll have to step in as her first handmaiden, won't you?' Miles said.

'I think so,' I said, feeling so full of happiness that I could hardly think.

'Well then, you should probably get some beauty sleep.'

I got into bed in a daze. Miles hopped in at the other end and flicked one of my toes.

'Mary is so sappy anyway,' he said. 'You'll make a much better Carnival Queen.'

29

The Parade

The thing is, I should say this now: I didn't ever think any of this would happen. And you can't blame me for what happened, because it isn't my fault at all. Any of it.

The morning of the carnival was the happiest few hours of my whole life. Aunt Maria put my hair in some of her curlers to make it look proper, and bought me some special glitter to put on my cheeks. I was a bit burned from the day at the beach and looked a bit red in my dress, so she put some powder on my arms and shoulders.

When I came down to breakfast, even Jean said I looked nice, 'like a proper young woman', and Winnie was absolutely furious all morning, crashing all of the cutlery around and stomping about saying that she would look after the hotel during the afternoon, since the carnival procession was going to be terrible anyway.

Miles was sitting at the other end of the dining room with Mrs Tiggy-Winkle, but I could tell that he was looking at me because every time I glanced over he pretended to look at something else.

It was the greatest day of my life. Better even than when Miles gave me my book of ghost stories and said he was my best friend.

Aunt Maria took me down early. I'd insisted on this to make sure I got there before Martha so that I could volunteer as replacement Queen. The town was already full of decorations for the procession – silver-foil fish were glittering from strings along the lampposts, and there were balloons everywhere. Mrs Hoolhouse was fussing about the float, worrying that the lettering on the banner wasn't big enough.

'Poor Mary,' she kept saying. 'Such awful luck. She would have made such a lovely Queen.' She gave me a bit of a disappointed look. 'I'm sure you'll be good too.'

I ignored this. I was going to be the best Queen the town had ever seen – I had spent all morning practising my wave.

The parade always begins just after lunch. It starts outside Mr Podmore's gates and finishes in the quay where the band is. The Queen's float is the last one, after the Scouts and the lifeboat men and the Women's Institute. I couldn't eat anything I was so excited, and I had a tummy ache from the nerves, but Aunt Maria insisted I have a few bites of a cheese sandwich so that I didn't faint in the heat.

The town band had started playing 'What Shall We Do With the Drunken Sailor?' – we could hear it from above as the people for the other floats began to arrive. Mayor Hoolhouse always toots on an old bicycle horn to sound the beginning of the procession. He was wearing his mayoral robes and necklaces especially for the occasion, and was fussing around the floats, making sure everything was tip-top.

The crowning happens at the quay and is always the big finale of the parade. Martha was in charge of crowning me and was already in a tizz in case she didn't do it right. I was in such a good mood that I told her I wouldn't even care if she put it on upside down. That seemed to calm her nerves a bit.

People started lining the streets all the way through the town and they were cheering and waving little flags. It was nearly time. I smoothed down my white dress, making sure everything would be perfect for when I got down to the quay, where I knew Miles would be waiting.

The town bell rang three, and Mayor Hoolhouse sounded the horn. The floats rumbled into gear ahead of us, rattling along the street, until finally it was time for us. The tractor started up, and with a few jerks we were off! People were cheering on all sides, singing and whooping and whistling as I went past. And when I waved they waved back!

We wound all the way around the town. I had to clutch onto my throne a few times, because the nerves in my stomach were so bad. But I kept on smiling, because soon I would be at the quay and Miles would see me!

There were so many people at the quay when we arrived I could hardly believe it. Everyone was there! Uncle Frederick and Aunt Maria and Peter Queen and Albert Fish and PC Nodder. Cheering away. I saw Miles, leaning up against a bollard, smiling. He was pleased. And it was all down to him!

Mayor Hoolhouse tooted his horn again. This was the moment! Martha had the crown in her hands, ready to put it on my head. The band struck up 'For She's a Jolly Good Fellow' and everyone sang along – even Miles!

I stood up, burning with excitement.

Suddenly everyone was quiet. The band stopped.

I couldn't work out what was going on. I thought at first that it was part of the ceremony, but a few people had their hands to their mouths.

'Oh no!' Martha said behind me.

I looked down.

There was blood on my dress. A huge great patch of it at the front. It was sticky and wet between my legs. I didn't understand. I couldn't work it out.

Mrs Hoolhouse rushed over, taking off her pink jumper and thrusting it at me.

'Here you are, dear, cover it up.'

Some people were laughing now. Some boys from the town. Scoffing and pointing and jeering.

Then I realised what had happened. I'd heard girls talking about it at school. The first time. The first time today. It was punishment, I thought. For Mary.

I felt like I might fall off the float.

I could see Aunt Maria trying to make her way over to me, but Uncle Frederick held onto her tightly.

Miles wasn't smiling any more.

I ran.

30

Bath Time

There was no one in the hotel; everyone was in the town. No one had followed me. I could barely breathe from the running and the horror. My dress clung to my legs, sticking to me. The blood had turned a rusty brown now.

I stood frozen in the lobby, gripped. The memory of it came to me in sharp, bright pangs. Uncle Frederick's hand as he stopped Aunt Maria. Mrs Hoolhouse's horrified face. The boys laughing. I was the spider under the glass now, with faces peering in at me from all sides.

I made it up the stairs to my room. The mirror was another enemy. I looked like something out of a horror film. I looked like one of the mermaids washed up on the beach. My hair was flattened to my face with sweat. The make-up Aunt Maria had applied so carefully had smudged. And the dress. How could there be so much blood? No one had told me.

I didn't even know what I was supposed to do. Would I bleed forever? How did other girls manage it? Stop it from happening? Why hadn't anyone told me?

I was too shocked even to cry. I could only pace, pace, pace around my room, trying to stop the thoughts. It was worse than embarrassment, worse than shame. I couldn't see myself ever getting away from it. What would happen when everyone got back to the hotel? How could I look at them?

There was a knock at the door. I stopped. I didn't even dare breathe. I couldn't have anyone come in. If someone came in I would die. But my voice wouldn't get out; nothing would work.

Miles stood in the doorway.

There was no use even trying to cover the dress now. He looked at it, not even pretending he wasn't.

'Well, no one's going to forget that in a hurry,' he said.

It was too soon for jokes. He might as well have peeled off my skin, it stung so much.

I was shaking too much even to hide it.

'You should have heard the town after you left,' Miles said. 'Mayor Hoolhouse is furious.'

'Don't, Miles,' I said. 'Please don't.'

He walked towards me and I flinched away.

'Hey,' he said. 'Come on, it's funny.'

'No.'

'It is! It's WAY better than giving everyone the finger.'

I wanted to beg him to be quiet. I would have done anything to make him stop.

'Didn't you know?' he asked, looking down at the dress.

'No.' Why was he talking about it? Why was he asking me about it?

'What does it feel like?' He circled me.

'Like being stabbed.'

He couldn't take his eyes away.

'Can I see?' he asked.

I stared at him. Thinking he must be joking.

'Shut up,' I said.

'I'm serious.'

'No,' I said.

'Come on, don't be a baby about it! It's only a bit of blood. It'll be like the murder games. You lie still, like this.'

He pushed me gently onto the bed.

I can't even say what I felt. Frightened that he was playing a trick on me, but something else too.

He arranged me on the bed, and pulled up my dress around my hips.

'Stay still!' he ordered when I tried to push it back down again. 'You're murdered, remember?'

I was trying not to shiver, to stay still as he went about his examination.

He was fascinated, glued. I felt sure he would pull back, but he leaned in closer, closer, closer. I could feel his breath.

'What the hell are you doing?'

The voice cut through the room like a scalpel, cutting deeper than anything Miles was doing.

Miles pulled back, but it was too late.

Winnie was wearing a bathrobe, avocado green. The disgust on her face was like nothing else.

'Get away from her,' she said. Miles took a step back. I sat up and pulled my dress back down. I stared at the carpet.

'You little pervert,' she said to me. 'Wait until I tell your uncle!'

'Winnie, please don't,' I said.

'And you!' Winnie said, pointing at Miles. 'Your mother! I don't think she'll be very happy when I tell her what's been going on. I knew there was something about you two. It's not right.'

'They're all in town,' Miles said, calm, calm, calm.

'They'll be up soon enough.' She looked at me. 'Mark my words. They'll be up soon.'

'Please,' I begged.

'Do yourself a favour and get out of that filthy dress before they get here,' she sneered. 'You're not an animal.'

Miles didn't say a word.

It was the smile that did it. She couldn't help herself.

'Dear, dear, dear,' Winnie breathed. 'What will your Uncle Frederick say?'

As I said. It all happened so fast.

She turned down the corridor to take her bath, practically skipping, thrilled that in a few hours she would have me once and for all.

Miles grabbed me. 'Which room is she in?' he asked.

I was in a daze.

'What room is she in? Quick, we don't have any time,' he said again.

'She uses eight sometimes,' I said. 'Aunt Maria lets her have a bath after work so she doesn't have to go home. She'll be getting ready for the regatta party later.'

'Is there a spare door card?' he asked.

'It would be in the lobby, behind the desk.'

'Get it,' Miles said. 'Now.'

I didn't know what he was going to do. I promise I didn't.

I rushed down. Everyone was still in the town. I grabbed the card.

Miles was waiting outside room eight.

'What are you going to do, Miles?' I said. 'She'll go crazy.'

Miles slotted the card in. The little light went green.

The bathroom door was ajar, with steam curling out of the crack. I pulled at Miles's jumper, but he brushed me off.

Then the memory falls into pieces, like a broken mirror.

The bathroom door opening.

Winnie in the bath, trying to cover herself, yelling for us to get out.

Miles silent, moving quickly.

Miles grabbing her by the legs, yanking them upwards.

Her head disappearing under the water.

Her elbows banging against the bath.

Her hair in her mouth.

So many bubbles.

Eyes.

Feet kicking.

Hands grabbing at a wet shower curtain.

Eyes.

It didn't take long until she went limp and her hands slipped back into the bath.

After he was sure, Miles dropped her legs back down. His blond hair plastered to his forehead, his eyes shining.

He turned to me and grabbed me by the shoulders. I couldn't take my eyes away from Winnie. The room was still steamy.

'What did you do?' I said.

'You're not going to be silly about this, are you?' he said.

I had no answer.

'You see that we had to do it, don't you? She would have told Mother, and your uncle.'

All I could think of was the *Who's Who*. The man who killed his wives in the bath by pulling up their legs.

'Go back to your room,' Miles said. 'I'll go back to mine.'

I couldn't breathe. 'What about . . . what about . . .?'

'We'll leave her here. No one will come up, will they?'

'They will eventually.'

'I'll work it out,' he said. 'I'll work it out if you go to your room and change. Then go downstairs and pretend it never happened.'

31

Eiderdown

I was sick in my bath, and had to get out and run a new one. I changed into my Vlad T-shirt and my old skirt. I put my dress in the bin.

When I went down to the lobby, everyone had come back to get ready for the party. Uncle Frederick and Aunt Maria barely glanced at me, they were so embarrassed.

I sat in the parlour as everyone tried to be kind. Even Jean didn't say anything.

'You poor thing,' Dorothea said, patting my

hand. 'People will have forgotten it by tomorrow.'

I hardly knew what she was talking about. The carnival seemed like nothing now. All I could think of was Winnie, going cold in the bath upstairs.

The party would be in the Town Hall. Everyone would be going. They seemed to understand that I would rather go to bed early and stay in the hotel. No one questioned it. Miles told his mother that he was feeling a bit sick and could he please go to bed. She had already got her flowery party dress on by then.

'Do you want me to stay with you, precious?' she asked.

'No thank you, Mother,' he said, sweet as sugar. 'You go down and enjoy the party.'

'Such a good boy,' she said, kissing him.

When everyone had gone down to the Town Hall, Miles came to my room.

He sat on my bed. He was wearing some pink leather gloves that belonged to his mother. I would have laughed, if I hadn't felt so sick.

'They'll find out,' I said.

'No, they won't,' he said. 'What about the other girls?'

'What other girls?'

'The mermaids. They won't think twice, will they? If another mermaid is found. They'll never think it was us. They'll think it was the murderer again. They never thought it was George Brain anyway. Not really.'

I didn't believe him, but I didn't see that I had much choice.

I didn't want to go back into number eight. Miles had to pull me in, my heels burning along the carpet.

I half expected Winnie not to be in there, as if she might have woken up and walked out.

Her body was wrinkled from the water.

'Come on,' Miles said. 'Help me. Get the eiderdown from the bed.'

We spread it out onto the bathroom floor, and Miles hooked Winnie under her arms and hauled her out of the bath.

Her skin squeaked. She had a tattoo. A dragonfly.

He flopped her onto the eiderdown and rolled her up, her wet hair sticking out of one end.

'I can't do it,' I said.

'Yes, you can,' he said.

'Why did you do it, Miles?' I said. My voice was louder, I was shouting now. 'Why did you do it?'

Miles was angry.

'I did it for you!' he said. 'What would have happened to you if your uncle had found out? I've done you the biggest favour of your life. You hated her, didn't you?'

'Yes, but –'

'Well, there you are then. You know we couldn't be friends if they found out. Mother would never bring me back here.'

I couldn't bear to think of it.

'You should be grateful.'

I didn't feel grateful. But there was something else, mixed in with all the nerves and the fear. Not pleased, not grateful, but relieved maybe. Miles had saved us, it was true. And he had done it for me.

We needed to get rid of the body.

'Now stop being such a weed and help me with this.'

It took us a while to get her out into the garden. We had to go slowly, because Miles was stronger than me and the eiderdown kept slipping out of my hands.

We pulled her along the grass towards the cliff edge, like a snail curled up nice and snug in its shell. I peered over the cliff.

'What if she gets caught on the way down?' I said.

'Then we'll climb down and give her a kick.'

He laid her down on the grass, held onto the edge of the eiderdown and then yanked it back. It unrolled quickly, gaining momentum down the hill, until the body emerged, white in the moonlight, and dropped off the cliff edge. Miles stood holding the eiderdown. We heard the splash.

I couldn't look down. But Miles did.

'Gone,' he said.

32

Smugglers' Cave

She was found this morning. She hadn't gone far.
Aunt Maria was hysterical, so Uncle Frederick
made her take a sleeping pill and go to bed. Even
Uncle Frederick was upset about it. He couldn't
concentrate and let the phone ring in the lobby
without answering it.

'Poor George Brain,' Dorothea said. 'It can't
have been him after all.'

PC Nodder was all over the hotel, asking
questions. Miles and I had both been in bed all

night, of course. He barely even asked us.

Jean kept clutching a handkerchief to her face even though she wasn't crying, but Dorothea wept openly. 'That poor girl,' she kept saying. 'That poor, poor girl.'

Mrs Tiggy-Winkle is taking Miles away tonight, a day early. She says that the police in the hotel are upsetting her little Miles. Miles is putting on a good show of being sad and helpful. I can hardly speak.

We had organised to meet down by the beach. Miles was late because it took him ages to persuade his mother to let him out of her sight.

We sat in silence.

'You won't tell, will you?' he said.

He knew I wouldn't tell.

'We're in this together now. We can't tell anyone,' he said.

'What if they find out?' I asked.

'PC Nodder? Fat chance. She'll go in with all the other murders, and we'll go home, won't we?'

Home. I thought of my parents' flat in London. I wondered who lived in it now.

'And then we'll both come back next summer, won't we?' he said.

'Your mother won't let you,' I said. This thought upset me almost more than us being found out.

'She will. She always lets me do what I want.'

I looked across the beach to the cliffs. The ruined fortress looking out to the sea, and the crack in the rock that lead to the smugglers' caves.

And then I thought, what an idiot. Of course! The caves.

Why hadn't I thought of the caves?

'Miles,' I said, grabbing him. 'The smugglers' caves.'

'What?' he said.

I pointed to the crack in the cliff ahead of us.

'George Brain was always talking about passages under the town. The smugglers, they used to use the caves to get rum in and out of the town. What if that's how the murderer got the bodies into the sea without anyone seeing?'

Miles looked at the cave. It was quite a swim away.

'Let's see,' he said.

It took us a while to swim with our clothes on and our shoes in our hands. The water was freezing, and I couldn't help but think of George Brain's kraken slinking around below us, and the sailors who snuck up behind the sirens and strangled them. Miles was a stronger swimmer than me, but he went slowly as I gulped down the water.

'Don't panic,' Miles said as I started to get tired and lose my breath. 'It's the people who panic that drown.'

I kept calm for Miles, swimming the last few feet quietly, even though my arms ached.

The crack in the rock face was narrow, just wide enough for one person to slip through it. But the cave behind it was enormous, far bigger than either of us had expected. The ceiling must have been thirty feet above us. It looked more like a church than a cave. Miles hoisted himself onto the rocks, and hauled me up after him.

'This is weird,' Miles said. There were candles on the rocks, hundreds of them, and iron candelabras fixed onto the wall. Miles hunted around. 'If there are candles,' he said, 'what are the chances there'll be something to light them with?'

He found a stack of matches behind a rock, brand new.

The place rose up around us in the candlelight, all ridges and shadows. Like the black, ribbed mouth of a basking shark. Water dripped from the ceiling. I shivered in my wet clothes; it was freezing, the kind of cold that crept right down into you.

In the light you could just see a gap in the rock face between two stones.

Miles lit a candle and passed it to me.

'Should we have a look?' he asked.

Well, I didn't really have much choice, did I?

The gap was so narrow you had to walk through it sideways, your chest and back brushing the stone. I didn't like it. What if a rock fell? We'd be trapped in there forever, no one knowing where we were.

After a few metres the passage opened out

into a little cave, which forked into two separate passages.

'Let's go back, Miles,' I said. If our candles went out, we'd never be able to find our way back again. 'We might get trapped.'

'Don't be a baby,' Miles said.

We took the left fork first – this passage was less narrow; we could walk along it side by side. Candelabras were fixed on the walls here too. We walked for ages, the ground shifting uphill, water dripping onto our heads.

'We must be under the town,' Miles said. I thought of everyone above us, scurrying around on the cobblestones in the sunshine while we moled around underneath them.

Up ahead was a dead end.

'Hang on,' I said. 'Is that a door?'

It was. Wooden, with an iron latch. I could hardly believe it.

I grabbed Miles's hand as he reached for the latch.

'Come on,' he said. 'Don't you want to know?'

He was right. I did.

'You go ahead,' I said.

He rolled his eyes.

The door wasn't locked – it opened easily – but there was something in front of us: a thick swag of fabric. Miles pulled it up and ducked underneath it, and I followed.

It took my eyes a moment to adjust to the light.

We were in someone's house. A huge stone hall. There were weapons all over the walls, swords and axes and shields, and a wooden staircase covered in dragons baring their sharp teeth. Behind us, the huge tapestry had fallen back into place, covering the door to the cave.

'Where are we?' Miles asked.

I couldn't think. I was sure we were in the town somewhere, but I'd never seen anything like it. I tiptoed over to the latticed window to get my bearings. A garden full of hydrangeas rolled down to a castellated wall, and beyond it you could see the whole town.

'It's Podmore Hall,' I said. We were in Mr Podmore's house.

'We should go,' I said. 'Now.'

317

Miles ignored me.

The place was filthy. Thick with dust.

'Please, Miles,' I whispered.

'There's no one here,' he said.

'How do you know?'

'Look!'

He pointed at a doorway covered in cobwebs.

'He might be upstairs,' I said.

Miles brushed the cobwebs from the doorway and walked into one of the rooms. I hesitated.

'Woah,' he said. 'You should come in here.'

It was a dining room – or, it looked like it might once have been a dining room. A long wooden table ran down the middle of it, an inch of dust on it and covered in hundreds of yellowing jars.

Miles picked up one of the jars – it had a fingernail in it, painted red.

I felt a bit dizzy, but I couldn't stop looking. It was even more gruesome than the Ripper girl with her guts pulled out.

'Look at these!' Miles said.

I looked closer. Each jar had something floating inside it. Stolen from the mermaids.

In the middle of the table was a bowl, full of Thunder Stones. Miles took one and rolled it between his fingers, looking over the jars again.

'He's been doing this for years,' Miles said. He sounded impressed. 'I'll bet you a million pounds Mrs Queen is in one of these.'

'It's horrible,' I said.

'You know what this means, don't you?' he said.

'No. What?'

'We've done it. We've solved the murders. Podmore will go down for them all, Winnie included.'

My heart beat faster. Miles was right. We would get away with it! We would bloody get away with it!

But there was something wrong.

'But where is he?' I asked.

Miles rubbed his fingerprints carefully off the jars with the sleeve of his jumper.

'We should probably go, Miles,' I said.

'What's the rush?' Miles asked, peering in at a floating pair of false eyelashes. 'He's obviously not here, is he? No one's been here for ages.'

He had a point. The place had the same dank, unused smell as the pillbox, with the tang of whatever chemical was in the jars pushing up into my nostrils.

Miles began to walk around the house, with me trailing behind him, trying not to seem weedy. I was sure Podmore would spring out at us.

We walked into the next-door room. The tartan curtains were drawn, so Miles tried the light: nothing. It must have been a ballroom at some point – there were gold mirrors on the walls and a glass chandelier hanging lopsidedly in the middle of the ceiling. The room was bare except for a single, worn sofa facing an old television. There was a plate on the floor next to it, with the dried-up remnants of dinner hardening on the surface.

We tiptoed around, room by room, and each room was larger and emptier than the last. One bedroom had nothing inside it but a wardrobe full of fur coats; another had a four-poster bed with no mattress. The smallest upstairs room seemed to be Podmore's. It was a bathroom with a single, sheetless bed pushed into it at an angle.

There was a ring of scum around the bath, and the water in the toilet had dried up.

Next to the bed were dozens of screwed-up bits of paper. Miles leaned down to pick one up.

'Dear Mr Queen,' he read. 'It has come to my attention that you have begun selling white chocolate mice in your shop. I thought I made it quite clear how I felt about this particular confectionery. Mice are filthy creatures and not befitting of the nature of the town. I expect you to cease selling them with immediate effect. William Podmore.'

'I love chocolate mice!' I said.

Miles picked up another bit of paper, and another, reading through them.

'They're all the same letter,' he said. 'About the mice. Look.'

He passed a couple over to me.

'They're different,' I said.

'No, they're not,' he said. 'They're the same, word for word.'

'Not the letters,' I said. 'The writing.'

Miles peered over to look at what I was seeing.

'You're right,' he said.

We smoothed out all the papers and looked: on each one the writing looked different.

'Do you think he's trying to copy someone's handwriting?' Miles asked. 'Why?'

That I couldn't answer.

We walked back down the stairs.

'But why isn't he here?' I asked.

'He must have done a runner,' Miles said. 'After the police started sniffing around.'

'But it can't be the first time the police have come! He's been doing this for years –'

'Shhh!' Miles said suddenly.

'What?' I said.

'Do you hear that?'

I listened.

'I can't hear anything,' I said, starting to feel nervous.

Miles tilted his head.

'It's humming,' he said.

I listened again. He was right: a low, electrical hum was coming out from behind a closed door next to the dining room.

'We need to go,' I said. 'Let's go now.'

But Miles was already creeping towards the door.

I grabbed at his arm.

'Stop it, Miles.'

He shook me off and went for the doorknob.

It was a kitchen. As sparse and damp as the rest of the house, the wallpaper peeling off in strips. The fridge door hung open.

At the far end was a freezer chest. The low, rumbling hum was coming from it.

Miles stared at it.

'Why don't you open it?' Miles asked.

'No way,' I said.

'Come on,' Miles grinned. 'I dare you.'

I thought of Mary Pearcey all tangled up in the nettles and thorns after one of Miles's dares.

'Don't be a baby,' he said. 'Double dare.'

I walked up to the freezer, with its horrible throbbing hum.

The latch of the handle was stuck.

'I can't do it,' I said. 'It's frozen shut.'

'You didn't even try. Use both hands.'

My back was to Miles, so I squeezed me eyes shut and yanked at the door. It came away with a *thock*, and I could feel the cold rising up from it. I opened one eye.

He was covered in frost. Eyes like frozen fish. The sweetcorn and frozen peas all torn open. A sweetcorn kernel nestled in the corner of an eye socket.

Miles ran up beside me.

'Shit,' he said.

He looked older than I had imagined. Long grey hair and long yellow nails. He was wearing a red jumper.

'Look,' Miles said, pointing to the door of the freezer.

It was covered in long, thick scratches. They had torn the plastic lining.

'He was put in here alive,' Miles said.

I let the door slam back down.

'We need to get out of here,' I said.

Miles didn't disagree this time.

We ran back to the hallway and yanked up the tapestry.

It was pitch black without our candles, but we ran down, down, down as fast as we could, running our hands along the damp walls for guidance.

Suddenly our fingers hit thin air: we were back in the smaller cave. I reached out to feel Miles; he was next to me, warm. He felt along the wall for the opening.

'It's this way,' I said, pulling him in the direction of the smugglers' cave.

Miles didn't move.

'Miles,' I said, tugging at him. 'Come on, let's go. Please.'

'Where does the other passage go?' he asked.

'It doesn't matter.'

'Doesn't it?'

'I don't care!'

'Aren't you curious?'

'It's too dark, Miles,' I said. 'Something could happen to us.'

'Don't be a baby,' he said.

Suddenly I could feel Miles close to me, his face hovering a few inches from mine, his breath hot on my face. He groped for my hand and squeezed it.

'Come on,' he whispered, and pulled me down the other passage.

I knew we'd regret it. I knew we would. But it was too late, because Miles had opened the door.

33

Home Sweet Home

It was like opening the freezer chest. The cold rising to meet me. Ice reaching down into my throat.

Miles didn't recognise the room, but why would he? He'd never been in it before.

The door was behind a bookcase full of thrillers and army books and an old certificate that said 'Hotel of the Year'.

Uncle Frederick was sitting behind his desk, as he always is. He didn't even look surprised to see us.

His face was redder than usual, but his knuckles were white.

'What have we been doing then?' Uncle Frederick said in his most uncly, jolly voice, as though he'd just come across us in the lobby.

Miles looked around the room, trying to work out what was going on. It was the first time I'd ever seen him look unsure.

'Are we in the hotel?' He was looking at me. I didn't dare answer.

Uncle Frederick smiled, his lips sticking to his yellow teeth. I felt like I was curled up on his dry tongue, ready to be chewed up.

'You two have been nosing around again then?' Uncle Frederick said. 'Poking around in the dark like a couple of crabs. Poke, poke, poke.'

He smoothed his greasy hair back onto his skull.

'And we all know what happens to little crabs who get caught, don't we? They get their claws twisted off.'

I could see his nose hair, blowing in and out on his ragged breath.

Miles glanced at the door.

'No use running,' Uncle Frederick said. 'No use running now.'

One purple eyelid was twitching. Twitch, twitch. Twitch, twitch. I couldn't stop looking at it. It seemed to twitch in time with my heartbeat. I wanted to reach out to Miles, to hide behind him, but he seemed to have taken a few steps away from me.

There was a fountain pen on Uncle Frederick's desk. Gold and ribbed.

And then all the screwed-up letters made sense. It wasn't Podmore copying someone else's handwriting, it was the opposite: someone trying to copy his. To keep Podmore alive, to make the town think he was alive while he was lying in the deep freezer with the peas and sweetcorn.

Uncle Frederick tapped his fingers on his desk like a spider. I thought about them wrapped around my neck.

'You're a clever little thing, aren't you?' he said, looking at me. 'Not half so clever as you think you are, though. And you –' He looked at Miles.

'Mummy's boy, getting involved with things that don't concern you.'

Miles bristled. 'We'll tell the police,' he said. 'We'll tell them you did it. That you put Podmore in the freezer.

'And what if I did?' Uncle Frederick said, white spit gathering at the corners of his mouth. 'What if I did shove him in there? He wasn't a nice man, was he? Killing all of those poor girls. I'm sure I'd be a hero, if I'd done something like that.'

'He can't have killed them all,' I said.

'What?' Uncle Frederick said.

'I saw him,' I said. 'He's been in there for ages – the freezer was almost frozen solid. He's been in there for a long time. From before this summer. He can't have killed all of them. He was dead.'

I had him there. Uncle Frederick sniffed, sucking in his nose hairs.

'I'm only saying what the police would say,' I said, feeling clever.

'What the police would say?' he said. 'I'd be worried about what the police would say about you two.'

Miles shifted next to me. I had put my foot in a trap and it was about to snap around my ankles.

'Poor little Winnie,' Uncle Frederick said, with a gleeful smile. 'I have to say, I was surprised when she turned up on the rocks this morning. With George Brain in the morgue I was home and dry for the others, but Winnie . . . well, she complicates things. Luckily I was at the regatta celebrations last night with plenty of witnesses, but you two . . .'

The trap snapped shut.

'You weren't very careful, you know,' Uncle Frederick said. 'The room was a mess. I expect you will have left all sorts of things behind on that eiderdown. But, by all means, go to the police and tell them whatever you like. I'm sure they'd be very interested to hear what I have to say about you in return.'

'We don't know what you're talking about. We haven't done anything,' Miles said. His voice sounded high, boyish. Like when he wheedled with his mother.

'Don't insult me,' Uncle Frederick said. 'I'm not an idiot like PC Nodder. I've been doing this since before you two were born.'

'But why?' I asked.

'Why?' Uncle Frederick said. 'Why not? Podmore had a . . . peccadillo. And if a few of us helped him indulge it over the years, for our own benefit, what's the harm in that?'

'A few of you?' I asked.

'Come on now, catch up! I thought you were the clever clogs!' Uncle Frederick said. 'You must have thought . . . all those girls going missing over the years. All those "accidental" drownings. Poor old Peter Queen's wife. Peter feels very guilty about that – never quite got over it, if you ask me.'

'I don't believe you,' I said. 'Why would he do that? Why would any of you do it?'

'Oh, don't be such a little priss,' Uncle Frederick said, spit on his lip. 'Why do you think Peter Queen can afford his sweetshop? Because Podmore let him have it for free, so long as he sold the right things and did the odd job on the side. Why do you think a man so incompetent as Hoolhouse is Mayor?'

'Hoolhouse!' I said.

'Oh yes, Mayor Hoolhouse was a very good friend of Podmore's a few years back.'

'You're lying,' Miles said. 'There's no way.'

'Isn't there?' Uncle Frederick said. 'You'd be surprised what people would do to live in a beautiful town full of flags and sunshine and with no litter on the streets. To run a little shop in that town, or be the Mayor of that town, or have a hotel in that town. My own father was awfully close to Podmore too, you know. My family wouldn't have had this hotel if it weren't for dear old Podmore.'

Uncle Frederick stroked his desk lovingly.

'For the sake of a few silly girls, it's not too steep a price.'

Uncle Frederick seemed calmer, almost giddy with the admission. Like he was telling us a joke.

I thought about the girls at the bottom of the sea, with their eyes out and the Thunder Stones in their mouths.

'What about the stones?' I asked.

'Oh that!' Uncle Frederick giggled. 'Something Podmore liked to do, otherwise he said he heard the mermaids screaming when he closed his eyes. I thought I'd carry on with it. It's tradition!'

'But Podmore's dead now,' Miles said. 'So . . . why carry on with it at all?'

Uncle Frederick rolled his eyes, as though Miles was a dunce at the back of the class who had asked how to spell his own name.

'Podmore and I . . .' Uncle Frederick said, steepling his fingers, 'stopped seeing eye to eye.'

'How?' I asked.

'He felt I was becoming a little too enthusiastic. Reckless, he called it. He was a collector, you see – what they call an aficionado. Filling his jars with souvenirs. He was content to wait, years sometimes, for the right specimen to come along, whereas I enjoyed . . . other aspects. Queen, Hoolhouse and the others, they'd done him their favour and got out. But I stayed. I liked to help. But then Podmore felt that I was letting things get out of control. He was getting old, deranged. Started to imagine things. Ghosts. Things were weighing on his conscience. He was even talking about the police. Pretty rich, if you ask me! And after all I'd done for him! We had an argument . . .'

He spread his hands out, as though he was talking about a quibble in the supermarket, rather than stuffing an old man in a freezer.

'When did you do it?' I asked.

'A few months ago,' he answered.

'Why didn't you put him in the water like the others?' Miles asked.

Uncle Frederick tapped his finger on the side of his nose.

'Because,' he said, with a giggle, 'freezing keeps him nice and fresh. If they ever come after me, if that thick policeman starts getting ideas, then I'll shove him in the water. It will look like he's only just jumped in. We've all still been getting letters from the man, so as far as everyone knows he's alive. And with all those jars up at Podmore Hall, I think the police would put two and two together, don't you?'

It sounded like something straight out of the *Who's Who*. I was suddenly between the pages, rubbing up against the black ink with all the other murderers.

'Since he's been gone, I've been able to really enjoy myself,' Uncle Frederick said. 'But, honestly, it's not been the same. Not being able to talk about it with anyone, well, where's the fun in that? But you two . . .'

He leaned forward and smiled at us.

'Now you two are here, everything is different.'

'What do you mean?' I asked, everything cold, everything tight and icy.

'You two are like me, just like me. And we can do whatever we want now. Just think of it! You can come back next summer, and you can do whatever you like together. And I can teach you, like Mr Podmore taught me.'

I looked over at Miles. He didn't look surprised, or angry, or upset. His eyes were shining. His face was flushed. It went all the way down to his neck.

'My mother might not let me come back, though,' Miles said, his breath shallow.

'Oh yes, she will,' Uncle Frederick said. 'You'll make sure she does.'

There was a knock on the door. Miles and I jumped.

It was Aunt Maria.

'Oh!' she said nervously. 'I didn't know you two were in here! Miles, your mother is looking for you.'

34

What We Did on Our Summer Holidays

Everything in the lobby looked like it always had, but it felt different, I felt different, like my bones had been swapped for someone else's. I could feel the hard floor pressing up against my shoes, and the ornaments and dried flowers seemed to be looking at me and whispering. I grabbed for Miles's hand.

Jean sat in her usual chair, eyeing us up.

'Dear, dear,' Jean called to me with a little sneer. 'You'll be sad to see your friend go, won't you?'

'But I'll be back next year,' Miles said calmly. 'Then I'll get to see you again, Jean. I'm looking forward to seeing you again.'

Jean simpered in spite of herself. 'What a polite boy,' she said to Dorothea.

Miles's mother was bearing down on us, carrying their suitcases.

'Will we be all right?' I asked, holding his hand more tightly.

Miles turned. He was smiling, all teeth and eyes. 'We'll be all right,' he said. He leaned in and kissed my cheek. He smelled of the sea and of the wool of his silly jumper and of our summer.

'See you next year,' he whispered.

And he would.

Because what does any of it even matter anyway? Miles is my best friend, and he's a better friend than I'll ever have for the rest of my life. And next summer will be wonderful, because we'll be together again and we can play our games and no one will bother us and we can do whatever we like from now on. No one can stop us now, can they?

Because we have each other.

And our secrets are safe in the dark.

Yes, next summer will be wonderful.

Emerald Fennell

Emerald Fennell is a writer, actress, screenwriter and director. She studied English at Oxford University and lives in London. Emerald's debut children's novel SHIVERTON HALL (Bloomsbury) was shortlisted for the Waterstone's Children's Book Prize 2014 and was followed by its sequel, THE CREEPER.

Thank you for choosing a Hot Key book.

If you want to know more about our authors and what we publish, you can find us online.

You can start at our website

www.hotkeybooks.com

And you can also find us on:

We hope to see you soon!